LOST *and* FOUND

For Jill...
I hope you enjoy
my first novel!!
♡

LOST *and* FOUND

A story of faith, love and survival

J.C. LAFLER

TATE PUBLISHING
AND ENTERPRISES, LLC

This novel is a work of fiction. Names, descriptions, entities, and incidents included in the story are products of the author's imagination. Any resemblance to actual persons, events, and entities is entirely coincidental.

The opinions expressed by the author are not necessarily those of Tate Publishing, LLC.

Published by Tate Publishing & Enterprises, LLC
127 E. Trade Center Terrace | Mustang, Oklahoma 73064 USA
1.888.361.9473 | www.tatepublishing.com

Tate Publishing is committed to excellence in the publishing industry. The company reflects the philosophy established by the founders, based on Psalm 68:11,
"The Lord gave the word and great was the company of those who published it."

Cover design by Samson Lim
Interior design by Caypeeline Casas

Published in the United States of America

ISBN: 978-1-63367-745-6
Fiction / General
16.07.29

For the two Davids who have
had a significant impact on my life:
My father, David DuWayne Hewitt,
who is now in heaven but would have been so proud,
and my husband, David Lee Lafler,
who is simply my gift from God!

He didn't look like much in his dirty, tattered clothes
His fingernails were filthy and he had a runny nose

He missed two buttons on his shirt; his shoes were scuffed and worn
With laces dragging in the dirt and pant legs soiled and torn

But what seemed hopeless at a glance, was a very special child indeed
And given just a single chance, one other who would see his need
The "real him" might be born.

The possibilities were there, a mind and heart and soul intact
Beneath the shaggy, uncombed hair, if someone only knew that fact

And whose responsibility, to wonder or to even care
Did anybody want to see the child who lingered there?

It would be so easy just to leave him standing there without much hope
Pretending he would never grieve or someone else would help him cope with rejection and despair...

Who would ever even try to reach this child, and find a clue...?
Responding to his soundless cry and sticking by to see him through. Would you?

CONTENTS

PROLOGUE

At first glance, the bunched up clothing looked like a small, discarded scarecrow. A big, hairy rat crawled closer, sniffing along the body. He made his way to the scarecrow's head, partially concealed by a burlap bag, and crept closer, sensing warmth. The rat grabbed a potato peel from the garbage and nibbled, watching the movement that indicated shallow breathing. Without warning, the scarecrow sat up and jerked the bag away! The boy's eyes blinked open and slowly focused on the rat. When recognition finally registered, the startled boy sat up, pushed away the bags of garbage, and stood up, trembling on shaky legs. Tripping through the garbage, head and heart pounding out painful reminders of life, the boy put as much distance between him and the rat as he could manage.

He was stiff and sore, and he walked aimlessly at first, fighting the pain and feeling like he was watching himself move rather than doing it. Although late afternoon, the sun was still bright and he could see the water in the distance and skyscrapers shooting up against the blue sky. The area he walked in was filled with old buildings, crumbling sidewalks and mounds of garbage similar to the one he had just crawled from. Lifting his hand, he felt dried blood at the base of his skull. Tears rolled silently down his cheeks. A fuzzy image wavered in the background of his mind, but he couldn't bring it into focus. He rounded the corner and was instantly spotted by a gang of boys who started yelling at him and running toward him. Without hesitation, his "flight" response kicked in and he turned and fled as quickly as he could in the opposite direction. Darting in and out of doorways, around trash, and through empty buildings, he stumbled… never questioning why, never looking back.

The young woman in the hospital lay weeping silently. "Please, God, please let him be okay," she prayed.

1

DISCARDED

Running down the first alley he came to, the frightened boy ducked into an old building, scurrying into a back corner. The back door had fallen in and he was small enough to get behind it where he couldn't be seen. He held his breath, occasionally peering through a crack in the door to make sure no one was coming in after him. A few minutes later he saw the gang of boys running past the building, yelling out threats, obviously trying to figure out where he had gone. He slumped down behind the door, slowly catching his breath and trying to make out his surroundings. Where was he? Did he live here? Why did his head ache? Why was he alone? The questions poured into his mind, overwhelming him and making his head hurt even more. He focused on his immediate surroundings instead. He was in an old garage of some sort, with two big doors in the front and a door in the back that had fallen to one side (which he was currently hiding behind). One of the doors in the front was completely gone and the other one was hanging by some rusty framework that had broken away from the crumbling roof. Once enough time had passed that he didn't think the boys were coming back, he crept out from behind the door and over to the front of the building that overlooked the alley. It was windy outside, and it smelled awful! The alley looked run-down and seemed deserted to the boy, although he could hear traffic from a distance. Was it the police? Family? Friends? Should he try to make contact with someone who might help him? Suddenly he looked down at his own clothing. His shirt was ragged and he was missing a button or two in the middle. One elbow was worn almost through and there were holes in his jeans as well. His clothing was dirty from the trash pile, and the shoes he was wearing hurt his feet. He was pretty sure he smelled almost as bad as the alley! Would anyone be willing to help someone who looked like he did? The questions were pounding into his head like a hammer! He crept out the door and started tentatively down the alley. He kept a sharp lookout for the boys, glancing around constantly, heading toward the sound of faint music that he heard in the distance.

He saw old sheds and a couple of small, run-down houses, as well as a couple of empty lots where the houses were almost completely gone and the weeds grew taller than him. An old, wrinkled woman sat in a rickety rocker on the lopsided porch of one of the houses. She just stared straight ahead as the boy walked by. He saw an old gas station on the other side of the alley that was dirty and greasy-looking with a couple of old cars parked out back and several big, overflowing cans of garbage. After a couple of blocks, he could see that the music was coming out of a building up ahead covered in gaudy paint and neon lights. It was starting to get a bit darker now and the lights were beginning to stand out. He could also make out several people leaning up against the building smoking. They did not look like nice people at all, so the boy stayed away from that side of the alley. He was scared and getting tired again, so he ducked into the next empty building he came to, looking for a spot where he could rest. This building had been a tool shed at one time, as there were empty hooks and outlines where tools had been hanging on one wall. There was no door, but there were window frames stacked against one side of the building and an old rusty wheelbarrow leaning back in the corner. Empty crates and barrels were scattered around the shed. The boy found a crate and pulled it over in the corner behind the wheelbarrow. He could sit down out of sight there, and he could see the front opening through the rusty holes in the wheelbarrow. What was he supposed to do now?

His stomach was growling to the point of making him sick, and he had no idea when he had last had anything to eat or drink. Again the questions pounded inside his brain.

Who was he? Did he have a family? Was he lost? Why couldn't he remember anything! The boy suddenly heard someone coming and they were shouting. Were the boys coming back? No, this time one of the voices was a woman and she was yelling at a man! "You never get me anything nice," she screamed.

The man laughed and said rudely, "Well, I just bought you that bottle of water, didn't I? Maybe that's all you deserve!"

"Oh yeah," she yelled, "well, here's what I think about that!" She threw the water down the alley. It rolled right past the door of the shed where the boy was hiding. The woman huffed on down the alley with the man right on her heels, shouting about never buying her another thing. The boy waited, listening intently. As it got darker, he crept out from behind the wheelbarrow and peered out the door of the shed. He could just make out the bottle of water lying in the weeds along the alley. Slowly he walked over and picked up the bottle of water, looking both ways to make sure no one was around. He made his way back into the shed and stood in the corner gulping down the water. He knew he should probably save some, but he was so thirsty he drank it all! By now it was pretty dark, except for the trickles of light that came from the neon-sign building he had passed. He was afraid to stay outside, so he pushed a couple of crates together behind the wheelbarrow that he could lie down on and decided to stick it out there until morning.

He woke up with a start and looked around trying to find something that looked familiar. He couldn't figure out where he was and why he felt so stiff and sore. Then it all came rushing in… the trash pile, the boys chasing him, the smelly alley. His stomach was grumbling so loud he could hear it. He had to find something to eat! His hunger took over and he left the tool shed, heading further down the alley. He passed a couple more run-down houses and an empty lot where someone had made a pitiful attempt at planting a garden. It looked like a mass of weeds. He plodded on, feeling a sense of hopelessness that was overwhelming. After another block or two, he turned around and decided to go back and check out the garden. Maybe there was something there he could eat, even if it was only roots. When he reached the garden area, he checked carefully to make sure there was no one around. He waded through the weeds and started digging around for any plants that he might recognize. He saw a bit of red through the weeds and carefully separated them to find a tomato plant, with an actual tomato still attached! It was not quite ripe, but he ate it anyway. He had to get something in his stomach to stop it from rumbling. He looked for more tomatoes, but the rest of the plants were dry and brittle. He dug around a bit more and found what looked like the top of carrots. He pulled up a couple of the plants and was rewarded with several dirty, wrinkled up carrots. He wiped the dirt off on his pants and took a tentative bite. Yuck! It was awful! This was not what he needed. He climbed out of the weedy garden, sticking the wrinkled carrots in one of his pockets just in case that was all he could find. He headed back in the direction of the old gas station, thinking about the barrels of trash he had seen. As he walked along, he looked at the litter in the alley, hoping for something that was edible. He kicked at an old lunch bag and suddenly realized that there was something inside. He ran over and picked up the bag, feeling excited. Inside was the crust of a sandwich, a partially eaten bag of chips and a beat up apple. He wadded the bag shut and took off at a run, heading back to the shed. He hurried behind the wheelbarrow and opened his treasure. He gobbled down the bread crusts and chips and finished up with the battered apple. Nothing had ever tasted so good!

The boy realized he had to get help, or at least find a better area to hang out in. He left the shed and began walking toward what he thought sounded like traffic noise. He wound his way from alley to alley, keeping a lookout for danger. Sometimes he saw a stray cat or dog, and sometimes he spotted people here or there. The people he saw looked as bad as he did and some of them were even creepy-looking. He had to find something better than this! He walked for what seemed like hours and hours. As the daylight started to fade again, he started looking for a place to hide for the night. He found another deserted building that actually had a door this time! But when he opened the door, he saw several people huddled in a corner. They glared at him and he quickly backed outside, shut the door, and ran! He was so hungry and thirsty and afraid! Up ahead he saw a building that said "JOE's Tavern" in big, red letters and he slowed to a normal pace. Behind the bar was a trash container and he crept toward it. As he got near it, he saw something on the ground that looked like wrapped up food. In a hurry to see what it was, he didn't notice the man coming around the opposite corner. "Hey, get out of here, you punk," screamed the man. The boy snatched up the wrapper and ran. He ran for two more blocks before he stopped in a parking lot of beat-up, run-down cars. It looked like the lot had been abandoned, cars and all. Spotting a van with the front door hanging open, he crawled inside. The front seats of the van were ripped open and the sliding door of the van had been smashed in. The boy crawled further into the van and noticed that the very backseat was still intact. He crawled back and pulled himself up onto the seat. He hurriedly opened the wrapper he had snatched. Inside was a hamburger with only a bite or two out of it! It was cold and greasy, but it was something! The boy gobbled up the burger and decided this was going to be the best he could do for the night. He stretched out on the seat and fell into an exhausted sleep.

He was startled awake by someone screaming, "Alex, no!" He was disoriented, as it was still dark outside. Was someone out there? He crept over to the window and peered out, but all he could see was the junky cars. No movement and very little light made things look weird, but he didn't think the scream had come from outside. He realized he must have been dreaming, but hard as he tried couldn't bring the dream back. Still, he must have been dreaming about something that had happened in the past, right? Was he Alex? He lay back down on the seat and tried to go back to sleep. He decided that he must be Alex, and felt a bit better about at least knowing his own name.

In the morning he began another day like the others… searching for scraps of food, something to drink, somewhere to hide. One day he spotted an outside restroom at a run-down gas station and was able to sneak inside and actually use the facilities. He was able to wash his hands and scoop enough water in them to get a drink. It wasn't the cleanest place, but Alex tried to remember where it was located so he could come back if he needed to. Days and nights passed, and Alex was wearing blisters on his feet due to the tight sneakers. Still he wandered, not knowing what else to do. He looked like the dirty, ragged street urchin he was. If people noticed him, they ignored him, even looked at him disgustedly. No one he saw was friendly or even questioned why a boy his age would be wandering the streets.

2

HOME

The morning started like all the others, crawling out of his latest nighttime hiding spot, and starting the search for something to drink and some scrap of food. Alex, as he was now calling himself, spent most of the morning and early afternoon wandering and searching for food. Although he could always see the skyscrapers and water in the distance, it seemed like there were miles and miles of alleys and run-down neighborhoods to wander. He never seemed to get much closer to the city, which was probably for the best. Sometimes he would see familiar territory and realize he had actually been walking in circles! As Alex was wondering if this was the case today, he turned the corner and spotted the gang of boys who had chased him the first day he woke up. Before he could retrace his steps, the boys spotted him. The chase was on! Alex had no idea why these boys were chasing him, but he ran for all he was worth, down a street he wasn't familiar with, turning the corner and then picking up speed. He was small and quicker than the group of boys. At the end of the street he spotted a big white building and ran for the door. He had made a bit of headway on the boys, so they didn't see him duck into the building. Alex stood inside trying to get his bearings in the dim light. He was in a church! He silently walked to the back of the church, noticing some draperies along the wall that he could hide behind. As he stood against the wall behind the draperies, he noticed a door in the wall. Quickly he turned the handle, and to his surprise, the door opened easily. Inside was a flight of steps rising up to the floor above. Without hesitation, he started up the steps. When he reached the top, he passed through an alcove that led to a balcony of sorts. Standing there in the dark, he could see the layout of the church below. There were rows and rows of pews, with an area at the front that had a place for someone to stand and speak. Behind that a huge wooden cross hung on the wall. Alex was mesmerized! There was enough light for him to see the beautiful stained glass windows and know that this was a sanctuary.

Looking around the balcony, Alex spotted another door. Quietly he walked over and opened it. Another small, steep flight of stairs met his questioning eyes. He opened the door and started up, pulling himself by the railing in the dim light. When he reached the top, a small door opened up to a wondrous sight! This was a type of bell tower!

There was a huge brass bell suspended by ropes that could be manipulated to pull the bell through an opening in the roof. For now, the bell sat there taking up most of the room. Alex reached over and placed his hand on the bell. It was amazing. He looked around the bell at the rest of the small room. It had a low roof, with shelves along one wall that held a jumble of different items. At the opposite side of the room there was a small door. Quickly Alex made his way over to the door and opened it. He had to duck to get into the room, but once inside, he could stand upright. There were several rows of cots and lots of boxes. Peeking inside one of the boxes, Alex could see toys and books. Another held folded blankets and stuffed animals. It looked like stuff from a daycare. Briefly Alex wondered what a daycare was and how he knew about that, but suddenly he realized he had found a place to stay for more than one night. If he moved a few things around, he could make an area to sleep, and there were even blankets to use! Alex pulled a cot toward the area nearest the door and pulled a couple of blankets out of one of the boxes. He tentatively lay down on the cot. It was a bit short for him, but who cared! It was warm and safe and his! He wondered if anyone came into this room, and how often, but he doubted anyone would come in here. It seemed to be a storage room of sorts. Alex went back into the bell room and made sure he had closed the door leading in. He then made his way back to the little storage room and pulled the door almost closed. Enough light came in through the opening in the roof that Alex could see the stars. For the first time in many days, Alex felt happy. He crawled onto the cot, which felt wonderful after the other places he had been forced to sleep. Within minutes the exhausted boy was fast asleep.

Alex was dreaming again. He was warm and snug, cuddled up against someone. He could not see who it was, but he didn't really care. He felt warm and safe and content. Suddenly, someone pushed their way between them and he thudded to the floor! With a start, Alex awoke and found himself on the floor of the storage room. He had fallen off the small cot and just sat there recalling the bits of the dream he could remember. Who was he dreaming about, and why wasn't he with them anymore? He fought the tears and crawled back onto the cot. He pounded on the rolled up blanket he was using as a pillow and then lay there staring at the ceiling until, eventually, he fell back into a restless sleep. He didn't hear the creak of the cables at dawn as the bell was raised into the bell chamber ready to chime out the hours of the next day.

The next morning Alex awoke without the usual feeling of fear. He folded "his" blankets and slowly opened the door of the storage room. The bell was gone, and he wondered if the bell had been raised up above the church. Right now though, he had to locate a restroom. Alex slowly opened the door of the bell room, knowing he would have to go below to find one. Not finding one on the balcony level, he finally reached ground level and peered out from behind the draperies. The coast was clear, so he headed down the nearest hallway, spotting the restroom signs toward the end. He made his way to the men's room. Alex used the facilities and washed his hands and face with soap and water. He managed an awkward drink using his hands and decided that he needed to find an empty dish or bottle that he could fill with water. That way he would always have something to drink. He felt so relieved that he almost skipped as he headed out the door of the church!

Now that Alex had a place to stay, he could keep his wandering to the daytime, making his way back to the church by dark. He just had to make sure that the gang of boys never spotted him going into the church. He knew they had to be looking for someone to pick on, and he realized he was their latest target. Looking up at his "safe place," Alex almost cried. It was really beautiful! The church was white, with stained glass windows and big double doors, with lots of steps leading down to the street. Looking up, Alex could see the bell in the bell tower, with a shiny cross at the very top. It was the first building Alex had seen that wasn't falling apart. It looked sturdy, well-kept, and dependable. More than that, it looked Godly! *Now where had that come from?* Alex wondered, *and what did it mean?* Alex pushed the thought away and began his daily search for food.

3

REAL FOOD!

Alex squeezed in between two smelly, unwashed bodies in the food line. He didn't know what they looked like. He tried not to look at their faces. Their clothes were dirty and ragged like his. And they smelled. A *lot*! He knew he would be fortunate if they didn't notice him or realize how young he was. He was afraid they might try to take his food, *if* he got any. He tried to stand taller and appear uninterested in what was going on around him. His head was pounding to the beat of his heart.

Alex was famished. He hadn't eaten a real meal in weeks. He had only discovered this food kitchen by accident. Wandering around the city during the day, staying out of the more populated areas, he had tried to search in the poorer neighborhoods where he might not be noticed. He had no money and no clothes other than what he woke up wearing. His total possessions still consisted of a ragged shirt, dirty pants with a big ragged hole in one knee, and scruffy-looking sneakers that pinched his feet. He left them untied to give his feet a little more room, but his toes still ached at the ends. He felt so fortunate to have found this food place. The sign in the window said "Free bread and cheese every other Wednesday." Today must be Wednesday. Alex couldn't remember how he had learned to read, but today even that didn't matter. He had watched from the alley across the street for days wondering if it was true. After searching through garbage and living on scraps of leftover, half-eaten food, a loaf of bread and any kind of cheese sounded like heaven to Alex. This morning his perseverance had paid off. He had noticed that people were gathering outside the window with the sign and hurried across the street to join them.

After waiting for what seemed like hours to Alex, suddenly he was next in line! He rubbed at the ragged scab on the back of his head anxiously. Would the big lady handing out the food question him? Would she tell Alex he was too young to get food? The man in front of him grabbed an old plastic bag from a pile on the floor and held it open to the big lady. She barely looked at him as she reached into a large box and grabbed a package of cheese, while picking up a loaf of bread from the table beside her. She dropped them into the bag and reached back into the box for another. Alex didn't hesitate. He grabbed a bag and held it open in front of him, lifting it up as high as he could.

Plop! In went the cheese. *Whoosh!* The bread followed right behind it. Alex scurried out the door and across the street as fast as he could, expecting someone to grab him or the food at any moment!

He raced down the alley, around the corner and down the dirty, uneven street that ran behind rickety buildings and housing complexes. He knew his way from days of wandering the streets and nights of sneaking around in the shadows. He knew every trash container, every doorway, and every broken window along the way. He passed the back of the old booze restaurant, where one night he had found a hamburger with only one bite out of it, still half wrapped in a greasy piece of paper. He had devoured it in an instant and gone to sleep with more than usual in his grumpy stomach.

Right now though, Alex's face radiated with sheer determination as he raced toward the only place in this city where he felt safe. Suddenly, it loomed up before him. The white church had glazed, colorful windows that glowed warmly when the light struck them, and the cross reached high into the sky! Alex was home!

Entering the church cautiously, Alex crept up the first flight of stairs at the back of the church behind the velvety draperies. He peered over the balcony to the sanctuary below. He saw the warm glow of lighted candles and noticed someone praying silently in a pew toward the front. Without thinking about what he was doing, he stopped briefly on the balcony, bowed his head, and said a quick prayer for the bread and cheese. He tiptoed toward the back of the balcony where a small door led to another flight of stairs. He made his way to the top, clutching his treasure and panting deeply from the exertion. He opened the door and glanced quickly at the cables running from floor to ceiling and drew a deep breath knowing he was almost safe! Usually Alex felt great pride when he saw the bellroom. He had taken to polishing the bell when he could with some old rags he had found on the shelf. It made him feel like he was contributing to the church and had a reason for being there. Today, Alex quickly entered the small door behind the cables that led to his hideaway, because right now he had other things on his mind: mainly, his stomach! Still, he peered around carefully making sure everything was as he had left it. Even in his hunger, Alex was cautious.

Alex was still thankful that he had discovered the storage area. He had scooted a wooden crate into the corner and covered it with a clean piece of rag. Alex had dragged one of the cots close to the crate and covered it with several of the small blankets. He had rolled up a couple more for a makeshift pillow and finally had a dry place to sleep at night. It got pretty stuffy at times, but late at night he would open the door a crack and let in a little air. It certainly beat spending the night on the street!

Today Alex didn't notice much of anything. He crept to the small table and turned on the tiny battery-operated light that he had found on the shelf with the rags. Alex had painstakingly searched through a wrinkled, brown, paper sack full of batteries until he found some that worked. He even found a couple that he could use for spares. Alex silently closed the door. In the dim light, he carefully opened the bag and took out a whole loaf of bread and a package of processed cheese slices. He was so excited and so hungry that his hands shook. He opened the bread bag and took out two slices, then carefully closed it back up with the wire fastener. Next he unwrapped three slices of the cheese and placed them between the slices of bread.

Alex thought he had never tasted anything so fresh and clean and delicious! He ate the whole sandwich in a matter of seconds. It was so yummy! He washed it down with a few sips of water from a plastic container that he kept filled with water. Then he sat down on an overturned crate, staring at the loaf of bread and contemplating whether or not he should make another sandwich. Finally, his resolve to hoard the bread and cheese for other meals gave out and he fixed another sandwich. He only put two slices of cheese on this one and carefully counted the remaining slices in the package. Nineteen slices left. As he gobbled up the second sandwich, he picked up the loaf of bread and started counting the slices. Twenty-eight slices left. Alex quickly figured out that he could make fourteen more sandwiches, but he could only put one slice of cheese on nine of them and two on the other five. That meant that he could eat at least one sandwich a day until the next free food Wednesday was here. He took another sip of water, put it away carefully, turned out the light, and crawled around the crate to his makeshift bed. He pried the tight shoes off his feet and crawled onto the cot. His feet hung off the end of the bed a little bit, but Alex didn't mind at all. At least he could stretch his toes. It was warm, and his tummy wasn't empty for the first time in weeks! He hadn't slept much the night before, so he fell asleep almost immediately.

Suddenly, Alex felt the old familiar fear come over him. He heard a woman sobbing, "No, please, no," then a loud bang! She screamed, "Alex!" before the scene turned into sudden, total darkness. Now his head was pounding with pain and he was straining to see through the darkness, but all he could make out were shadowy figures. Someone hit him in the back of the head and he felt them grab him roughly and throw him over their shoulder before he passed out completely. Alex was smothering! Something was over his head and his arms were forced down at his sides. He must be Alex, right? Why didn't he know? Who was the woman? Why was he so afraid? Alex sat straight up. His forehead was beaded with sweat and he was trembling. The nightmare again! Why couldn't he remember more? Where had he come from? Alex lay back down and stared up at the rafters. Tears trickled down the side of his face. Would he ever know the answers to all the questions that swirled around in his head? Eventually, Alex drifted back into a light sleep. This time the images that came to him were happy ones. Alex was pulling old clothing out of a box and laughing! "I can still wear them," he shouted to someone just out of sight. Struggling into the old, worn clothing that had been his favorite at one time, and grabbing the old sneakers in the bottom of the box he headed toward that unknown someone and fell into a deeper sleep still smiling.

It was after noon by the time Alex woke and decided to do a little more exploring. The one good thing about being on your own was that you could do whatever you wanted, whenever you wanted to. However, along with being on your own came the heavy weight of responsibility. Alex knew he would give up his lonely existence for a warm, loving family in an instant. He *wanted* someone to tell him what to do and what was for supper and what kind of clothes to wear. And besides that, what about school? He must have gone to school. He knew how to read and figure out numbers. He just didn't know how he knew. Alex shook off the headache that always came when he tried too hard to remember. He had a full tummy and was feeling a bit adventuresome at the moment. He headed down toward the door that led outside.

Alex had learned in the last couple of weeks just how scary it could be after dark. Now that he had a place to stay, he kept his exploring of the city to daylight hours as much as possible. And knowing that he had some extra food stashed away took away some of the desperate anxiety that had been consuming him of late. Yep! Alex felt a little better for the first time since he had found himself alone in the middle of the day, in a filthy, rat-infested pile of garbage, with a scratchy, stinky bag over his head. He started walking toward a run-down shopping area that he had noticed. He didn't know how he would manage it, but somehow he needed to find a different pair of shoes or give up and start going barefoot!

4

THE SHOES

Alex peered into the dirty windows of the run-down shopping center. At one time it had been a variety store of some type, with brightly painted letters across the front. Now however, it was a battered, run-down secondhand shop. Two of the front windows were cracked and taped, and the only letters left across the front were *R* and *Y*. The rest of the letters were either smashed or had fallen off, leaving either a faded shadow or bits and pieces of broken plastic. Alex could see an old man carrying something from the back of the store. He walked around a low table that was piled with small boxes and stopped to add another to the pile. They looked like shoe boxes! All at once the old man glanced up and saw Alex peering in. He stood up and started toward the propped open door. Alex kept his eyes on the man and started edging away from the window. "What are you looking at, mister!" the man said in a loud, gruff voice.

"N-nothing," stammered Alex.

"Hey, you aren't one of that gang that was throwing rocks at me yesterday, are you, cause I'll call the police again and you'll be in big trouble. I've had about enough of you punks causing trouble around here!" The man coughed and wiped at his forehead with a handkerchief. "It's hard enough trying to fix this place up and make a living around here without you kids terrorizing me and stealing what little I have to work with. Do you hear me, kid?"

Alex nodded yes, looking down and scuffing his filthy shoes in the dirt. "It wasn't me," he mumbled quietly. "I don't belong to nobody."

"Well, what do you want then, I got work to do."

"I was looking for some sh-shoes," Alex said quickly. "It looked like you were stacking sh-shoe boxes."

"Well I doubt there's anything in your size, but take a look if you want. I'm right here watching mind you!"

Alex hurried over to the shoe boxes to look. He had no idea what size he wore or how he would possibly pay for shoes, but he couldn't resist at least looking. He sorted through used work boots, loafers, and sandals and finally spotted a couple of pairs of used sneakers that looked like they might fit him. He was so distracted by the shoes that he didn't notice the man coming up behind him until he spoke. "Do you know what size you are, kid?"

Alex jumped a mile and dropped the box of sneakers he had just picked up. He scrambled to gather them up, stammering, "N-not really, sir."

"Well, take your shoe off and let's just measure your foot then, boy, and find out." The old man picked up a metal thing shaped like a foot and squatted down to measure Alex's foot, as he painfully scooted his foot out of the filthy, worn, too-small sneaker he was currently wearing.

The man noticed how dirty Alex's foot was and saw the blisters at the end of his big toe. He suddenly wondered about this kid's age and circumstances, and as he looked up at Alex trying to guess, he caught the pained, embarrassed look on the kid's face. "Well, kid, looks like you need about a six or six and a half. I think the ones you were looking at just might fit."

Alex suddenly realized that this man was expecting him to buy some shoes, and nervously he put the box down and crammed his foot back into his old sneaker. "I w-was just looking, sir," he said. "I don't have any money."

The old man scratched his balding head and looked at Alex as he backed away from the shoes. It was obvious that this kid really needed some bigger shoes but had no money to buy them. Knowing that he might regret the offer and praying that he was doing the right thing, he said quickly, "Kid, are you willing to work to pay for the shoes?"

Alex turned back surprised and looked at the man questioningly. "Do you mean it, sir?"

"Well, I wouldn't offer if I didn't mean it, kid, but you had better be willing to work hard. I have a truckload of stuff out back that needs to be moved inside before dark. I don't have time to babysit you, and you need to be willing to keep at it till it's done. Can you handle that?"

"Oh, yes sir!" Alex said quickly. He thought about the newer, bigger shoes. "Yes sir! I'm sure I can do it!"

"Well, try those shoes on then and see if they even fit."

Alex struggled out of his shoe again and slipped his foot into the sneaker. There was plenty of room for his toes and the shoes hardly looked worn at all. He couldn't believe his luck! He carefully took off the shoes and placed them back in the box. He looked up seriously at the old man and said, "These shoes will be fine. Where's the stuff at, sir, I'm ready to get started."

He followed the old man out back behind the building, where someone had dumped a truckload of used clothing, books, and household items. It looked like a mountain to Alex, but bravely he picked up a box of books and started inside. The man showed Alex where to stack everything and left him to wait on another customer who was wandering around the store.

Alex worked for over an hour without stopping. He carried boxes and bags from the pile outside to a large storeroom at the back of the building. At first it seemed like he wasn't even making a dent in the mountain of goods, but little by little he whittled away at the pile. The old man, who said his name was Mr. Thompson, was busy sorting the stuff and placing it on shelves and tables in the store. Every now and then someone would wander into the store and

Mr. Thompson would stop to wait on them. Other than that, they both worked in silence. Alex kept thinking about how good it would feel to wear shoes that didn't hurt, and it gave him the energy he needed to keep going.

After about two hours, he realized that he had moved almost half of the pile! He was sweating and tired and thirsty, but nothing was going to keep him from earning those shoes. As he trudged back outside for another load, he met Mr. Thompson coming from a small room next to the storeroom. "How's it going, kid?" he asked Alex.

Alex glanced up quickly, worried that the man didn't think he was doing a good job or working fast enough or something and said, "F-fine, sir."

Unexpectedly, Mr. Thompson patted Alex's shoulder and smiled. "You are doing fine," he said. "Why don't you take a short break and have something to drink. Come on in here." He opened the door to the room he had just come out of, and Alex saw a small table with mismatched chairs, a cart on wheels that held a coffee maker, and an old refrigerator.

Mr. Thompson opened the refrigerator and pointed to cans of pop and bottles of juice. "Go ahead and pick something," he encouraged Alex as he lifted out a container from the bottom shelf. Alex tentatively chose a bottle of apple juice and turned to go outside. "Sit down here for a minute, son, you need a break." He opened the container he had removed from the refrigerator. "Have one of these. My wife baked them herself." He tipped the container toward Alex and the aroma of fresh baked chocolate chip cookies hit Alex square in the face. Alex didn't hesitate a moment longer. He reached in and took the first cookie he came to. It was huge! He bit into the cookie and closed his eyes as he savored the taste. A fleeting picture of a woman taking cookies out of the oven flashed through Alex's mind and he winced. She had her back to him and Alex couldn't see who she was, but she was laughing. A feeling of such longing came over Alex that he choked on the cookie. Suddenly, he realized that Mr. Thompson was looking at him strangely. He finished his cookie as quickly as he could, gulped down the juice, and almost ran back outside.

Mr. Thompson sat at the table wondering what he had gotten himself into this time. Mrs. Thompson was always telling him what a softie he was when he came across someone needy. She swore he gave away more than he sold. But Mr. Thompson knew need when he saw it, and this little boy was definitely in some sort of trouble. Where were his parents? Was he a runaway? Where did he live? What was his *name*? Mr. Thompson rose up slowly from his chair and pulled the cookies with him. He snapped the lid back on and returned them to the refrigerator. He rubbed at the ache his lower back as he returned to the store, unable to get Alex completely out of his thoughts.

Alex worked harder than ever. The cookie and juice had given him just the lift he needed. He wanted to finish this job, collect his shoes, and get out of here before Mr. Thompson started asking too many questions. How did you explain to someone that you didn't even remember your own name? Alex wasn't even positive that he *was* Alex. Even his name didn't feel like it belonged sometimes, but it was the only thing he could remember. He wondered about so many things, but he just didn't have the answers. Other than a few brief flashes like the one of the woman baking cookies, and the nightmares he had when he was sleeping, Alex had no recollection of anything. He had simply woken up one morning at the dump, on the outskirts of this city, struggling to get the bag off his head, only to find himself staring into the eyes of a big, fat, ugly rat!

Alex staggered into the storeroom carrying the last armload of goods. He had done it! The whole pile of stuff was now inside the storeroom. He glanced at a clock on the wall and realized it was almost five o'clock in the afternoon. He couldn't believe he had spent the whole day here! Alex walked into the store looking for Mr. Thompson, who was working up toward the front of the store. He walked up to Mr. Thompson and told him he was finished. Mr. Thompson put down his marker and price tags and headed back to take a look. He couldn't believe that Alex had managed to move that whole pile of merchandize, but sure enough it was all stacked neatly in the storeroom!

"Well, young man, it looks like you've done a fine job here."

"Yes sir, Mr. Thompson," Alex replied as he searched through his tattered jeans for something in his pocket. "I found this in the pile of stuff. I think it might be some money."

Mr. Thompson took the small leather pouch that Alex handed him in astonishment, realizing how easy it would have been for the kid to keep it. "What do we have here?" he said. Alex watched as he opened the pouch and poured out some coins. "These look old," he said. "I wonder where they came from." Mr. Thompson emptied out the rest of the contents of the pouch. Along with the old coins were some crumpled bills and small change. "Well, boy," he said, "I think you've found something here. Some of these coins are older than me! I don't know where that truck driver got this stuff, but I don't think he looked it over very good. I'm going to have to look into these old coins to see what they're worth, but you can keep the rest of it." He handed Alex back the pouch of money. "It's good to know there are honest kids around here too! Now let's go see about those shoes of yours!"

Mr. Thompson picked up the shoe box containing Alex's shoes from behind the cash register. "Let's get these shoes on, boy, and see how they look. Your feet have got to be killing you in those old things." He helped Alex pull off the filthy shoes and tossed them in a trash container without even asking Alex if he wanted to keep them. He sat down on the bench near Alex, pulling over a bucket of warm soapy water that he was going to wash up with, and a clean piece of toweling. He lifted Alex's sore, tired feet one by one and cleaned them gently, being extra careful around his big toes, which had started bleeding. Alex winced slightly when the old man hit a tender area but didn't say a word. Mr. Thompson reached into the utility apron that he was wearing and pulled out a pair of clean, white, tube socks. He pulled them onto Alex's feet and bent to help him into the sneakers.

Alex was so overcome that he didn't know what to say. There was a lump in his throat the size of a baseball, and he was afraid he might cry. Nobody had been nice to Alex in this city, or even noticed him for that matter. A gang of older boys had chased Alex, but they were screaming threats at him and just looking for someone to torment. No one had shown him any kindness. Now, he sat here with new socks and new shoes and a pouch of money in his pocket. He just couldn't believe it! Mr. Thompson was looking at him keenly, and he managed to stammer, "Th-Thank you, sir. I can pay you for the socks."

"That's quite all right, young fella," replied Mr. Thompson, "You've more than earned both the shoes and the socks. I never really thought I would get all that stuff inside today."

"Well, are you sure you don't want this money th-thing?" Alex stuttered. "It was in your stuff."

"You keep it," Mr. Thompson replied. "I appreciate your honesty, and that can be your reward."

"Well, th-thank you again, sir, I had better get going." Alex started toward the front of the store.

"Just a minute," said the old man, hurrying toward the back of the store. He turned the corner toward the storeroom and Alex heard the sound of a door opening and some rustling noises. Mr. Thompson came hobbling back carrying a brown paper sack. "Here are a couple of extra cookies and some juice. You really didn't have a proper lunch today. And listen, if you're interested, I could use a little help on Saturdays with some sweeping and window washing and such. Just come on by if you have time."

Alex's eyes sparkled with appreciation and anticipation at Mr. Thompson's words. *If he had time?* he thought. What a joke! Time was one thing that Alex had plenty of. And now he had himself a sort of job. He mumbled another thank-you and a quick good-bye and hurried out the front door. He wondered if Mr. Thompson had a clue what he had just done for him. Alex thought he must have found his guardian angel! Suddenly, Alex realized that he had a pouch of money in his pocket, a bag of goodies in his hand, and new shoes and socks on his feet. He started running as fast as he could toward his church so he could settle down and enjoy his good fortune. Somebody was definitely watching over him today!

In a distant town, a young woman made her way to the front of her own church. She knelt carefully in front of the altar and prayed again for God's wisdom and help. "Please watch over him, Father, and keep him safe for me." Tears fell silently as she rose to leave...

5

THE GANG

The shopping center that Mr. Thompson's store was in was about ten blocks from the church. Alex had gone about half of the distance when he suddenly stopped short in a panic. His good luck had just run out! Half a block up the street was the gang of boys who had chased Alex from the dump, and again one night when he was searching desperately for something to eat. That was the night Alex had discovered the church and hidden in the bell room. He had seen them around several times since, busting up lights and looking for someone to torment. He had always managed to find a place to hide and lay low until they found some other trouble, but here he was running right at them! And worse, they had spotted him! Alex ducked around the first building he came to and ran for his life. He darted in and out of deserted buildings and headed away from the church. No way did he want those boys knowing where he stayed. He spotted an old parking structure and headed toward the ramp. As he came closer, he noticed a small ticket building with a big "CLOSED" sign across the window. He could hear the racket the boys were making as they screamed obscenities at him to let him know they were going to beat the crap out of him. Alex was sweating and almost out of breath when he noticed the door on the ticket booth standing open. He didn't hesitate! He sprinted up the ramp, jumped into the booth, and quickly shut the door.

Someone had installed a latch on the inside of the booth, probably for security purposes, and Alex latched it fast and slumped down out of sight. He was breathing so heavy that he was sure the boys would hear him if they came in this direction. He peeked up under the "CLOSED" sign just as the gang rounded the corner. He could see them across the street looking around trying to figure out which way to go. "Where'd he go!" shouted a burly red head with a thousand freckles.

"This way," growled a thick black boy with a huge nose.

"Naw," said the redhead, "let's go this way."

"I said he went this way," snarled the black boy, right in the red head's face. "You sayin' I'm wrong, *Redman*?"

The rest of the gang formed a circle around the two. The redhead pushed the black kid back out of his face. "Quit lookin' for trouble, Jake. I ain't callin' ya a liar. I just thought he mighta gone this way." He stood up to Jake, but it was clear that the black kid was the leader.

"Well, I say he went the other way and that's the way we're goin'. He's probably hidin' again by now. The little snot always seems to get away. He'll be sorry if we ever catch him. I got plans for that little twerp. Let's get goin'." The gang headed down the street away from Alex.

Alex slumped back down in the booth with a sigh of relief. They hadn't even looked in this direction. They were too busy fighting and bullying each other. He'd have to sit tight for a while though. He couldn't take a chance of running into them tonight. He didn't even want to think about Jake and Redman and what they had in mind for him. He'd have to wait till dark and sneak back to the church. Thank goodness for the new shoes and socks. Alex couldn't imagine what might have happened if he was still wearing his tight, filthy, old sneakers. Thinking about the new shoes reminded Alex about the rest of his day. Even being chased by that gang of boys couldn't take away his feeling of good fortune. And besides, it had turned out okay. Alex pulled a cookie out of the bag that Mr. Thompson had given him. He was beginning to feel hungry again, even after having two sandwiches this morning. Alex thought he had gotten used to the hungry feeling, but after having some real food for a change, he was hungrier than ever. And he was thirsty too. He pulled out the juice that Mr. Thompson had packed with the cookies and took a sip. He wouldn't drink too much though. He needed to save some for another day. Who knew when he'd have another day like this?

While he was munching and keeping an eye out the window in case the boys returned, Alex pulled the money pouch out of his pocket. He *had* considered keeping it when he heard the coins jingle, but now he was glad he hadn't. Alex remembered the crumpled bills and was anxious to see just how much money he had actually acquired. Even a couple dollars would be a Godsend.

Alex dumped the change out of the bag and counted it. He picked up two quarters, four nickels, three dimes, and a few pennies. A little bit over a dollar. He shook the two bills out last. Carefully he straightened them out, not believing what he saw. The first bill was not a one dollar bill as he had thought. It was a *ten* dollar bill! And the second one that had been crumpled even worse was a *twenty* dollar bill! Alex could not believe his eyes. Thirty-one dollars and some pennies! He also had new socks, new shoes, cookies, juice, and, possibly, a job. All of that in addition to finding the food kitchen passing out bread and cheese this morning. Suddenly Alex knew without a doubt that someone was watching over him. Maybe he would just have to listen more during those services he heard at church. Maybe there was something to this God story he had heard bits and pieces of. It sure felt familiar!

Alex also realized that he had the means to purchase some hot food, after eating nothing but scraps and garbage for weeks. He had seen a little coffee shop somewhere around here that sold soups and sandwiches and fruit and stuff, and now he had some money to buy whatever he wanted to eat! That certainly beat scrounging through the garbage. Alex was so excited that he almost knocked the "CLOSED" sign right off the window as he jumped up to leave.

Alex peered out the window once more, but there was no sign of the gang. It was almost dark as he opened the door and looked around. He made his way to the street and headed in the direction that he thought would lead past the coffee shop and back toward the church, keeping a lookout for the gang.

6

THE CORNER CAFÉ

Alex found the coffee shop without any more trouble. A couple of blocks from the parking garage, he turned the corner and there it was. Neon lights spelled out "The Corner Café." Alex didn't hesitate. He walked in a sat down at the first table he came to. The place was small but clean, and Alex felt a little bit uncomfortable in his dirty, ragged clothes. His tummy was growling so loud by now that he pushed the feelings away.

A young waitress walked up to his table. "Are you waiting for someone?" she asked politely.

"No," Alex replied, "it's just me." The waitress looked a little skeptical, but she went ahead and handed him a list of available items. Alex already had an idea what he wanted, so he glanced down the list quickly until he found what he was looking for. "I'll have a bowl of tomato soup and a glass of milk please," he told the waitress.

"That comes with either crackers or cheese bread," the waitress informed Alex, "which would you like?"

"Oh, I'll have the cheese bread then," Alex answered quickly, thinking that cheese and bread seemed to be the food for the day. The waitress walked away to turn in the order.

Alex picked up the menu and quickly added up the cost of his dinner. "One dollar and ninety-five cents for the soup (and bread) and ninety-nine cents for the milk," he thought to himself. "That'll be two dollars and ninety-four cents plus tip." Just as Alex was wondering how he knew about tips, the waitress returned with his milk and soup. "The cheese bread will be just a bit longer," she said. "Be careful. The soup is very hot!" She stopped at another table where an elderly couple was sitting, to see how they were doing. Alex took a sip of the milk and a sniff at the soup. He stirred it carefully, and as steam rose from the bowl, he decided to wait for the bread.

Alex yawned. What a day he had experienced. In twenty-four hours he had discovered the food line, the shoes, the job, and the gang. For once Alex was actually looking forward to getting back to his little cubbyhole and crawling into his makeshift bed. He was exhausted! The waitress returned with some hot, crusty bread smothered in cheese and Alex forgot about everything else. The hot food tasted wonderful. He ate every crumb and wiped his mouth carefully with his napkin. Oh, for a hot bath and clean clothes!

But Alex wasn't going to be greedy. He was certainly more than grateful for this day.

He took out the ten dollar bill and laid it on the ticket that the waitress had left on his table. When she stopped to pick it up and clear away the dishes, she asked him how everything was. "It was very good," Alex replied with a shy smile, "thank you." She patted him on the shoulder and commented on his good manners as she walked to the back to make change. She was back in a few minutes, and along with his change, she brought Alex several chocolate dinner mints. "Come back and see us soon, okay?" Alex quickly counted out the money for a tip and left with a mumbled good-bye.

As he left the café, the waitress watched him go with concern. What was a young boy doing in this neighborhood all by himself? He was so dirty and ragged, and yet his manners told a different story. She wondered if he needed clothing and thought about all of the outgrown clothes and things that her mother had put aside for Good Will this morning. Her little brother had outgrown them before they had even been worn out. Maybe she would pick out a few things and bring them to the café in case he returned. She found herself hoping that he would.

Alex walked home nervously, keeping an eye out for the gang of boys who kept pestering him. He felt the pouch of money tucked down securely in the pocket of his ragged jeans, touching his pocket every few minutes to make sure it was still there. He clutched the wrinkled brown bag that held the juice and extra cookie that Mr. Thompson had sent with him, in his right hand. He worried a bit about the way the waitress kept looking at him, but he knew he must look awful. She probably thought he was going to steal something, just like Mr. Thompson had at first. Alex knew he had to find a way to get cleaned up and get some new clothes. He thought about all the used clothing in Mr. Thompson's store. He hoped he could work toward earning some things on Saturday. In the meantime, he was going to have to find a way to make himself look a little more presentable. By the time Alex reached the church, he was totally exhausted. He climbed the flights of stairs wearily and checked his area out carefully as he always did before going to bed. Finally he took off his new shoes and socks, stored his cookie and juice under the crate, and crawled into his makeshift bed. He was sound asleep before his head even hit the pillow.

That night Alex dreamed of shoes. He was searching in his room for a box, and he was so excited. He was looking for shoes again, but this time he was looking for a pair of shoes that he wanted to show someone. He found them in a box in his closet, tucked away with some raggedy old clothing that he had outgrown. He tried on the shoes and just barely got his feet inside. He tied them up and a big smile crossed his face. He knew he could still wear them (well almost)! The clothes were another story, and besides they were kind of smelly. He had to go tell…wait a minute, hadn't he had this dream before? Confused but still happy, he lost the thought as he drifted on to deeper slumber.

7

THE SERVICE

Alex slept past noon the next day. He fleetingly recalled a pleasant dream about shoes that flitted through his memory before it eluded him, and he smiled knowing that the nightmares had left him alone for once. He woke refreshed, feeling the heat from the sun streaming through the window of the bell tower. He yawned and stretched his arms as far as his little space would allow. Ouch! Alex's arms ached a little bit and his back was stiff as a board. All the lifting and hauling yesterday had stretched muscles that Alex didn't realize he even had. It was probably a good thing that he wasn't going back to Mr. Thompson's store today. Still, Alex felt a little jolt of excitement when he thought about having a real job to go back to. It made him feel responsible and needed somehow. As the bell chimed the noon hour, Alex thought about the first time he heard it. It was early in the morning, a few days after the night the gang had chased him through the streets. The noise had literally knocked him right out of bed. Now, after weeks of "living" here, the bell chimes were like music to his soul. They represented safety to Alex and were sometimes the only thing that "spoke" to him.

Alex crawled out of his cot and tidied up his blankets. Once again he wished desperately for a hot bath and some clean clothes. He sat down beside his crate and took a quick sip of water. Then he moved the water and flashlight aside and gleefully studied his "groceries." He actually had a choice of food items for breakfast! The grumbling of his stomach reminded him of the many mornings when he had nothing to eat.

He decided on the chocolate chip cookie and juice for breakfast, knowing that he could have a wonderful cheese sandwich for lunch or a hot meal for dinner if he wanted to. He lifted the little pouch of money and bounced it in his hand as he munched on the delicious cookie. He would have to be very careful about spending this money. He needed to make it last as long as possible. He finished the cookie and washed it down with the last drop of juice. Boy, a cold glass of milk would have been great with that cookie! Oh well, Alex was not going to complain. He was feeling pretty good at the moment, considering the last few weeks.

Alex heard murmurings from downstairs and realized it was the day when a lot of women gathered in the church to sing and pray. He now knew that it was Thursday and must be some type of ladies church group. Sometimes Alex would sit by the open door of the bell room and listen to the music. Often it made him cry though, and he would shut the door or leave the building. Today Alex was feeling brave. He opened the door and peered into the stairwell. When he saw that the coast was clear, he crept down the first flight of stairs and peered over the church balcony. The women were coming in and sitting in the front pews of the church. Then someone started playing the piano. Alex liked the piano music best of all. Before too long, the women started singing. It was a song about someone knowing my name. "He knows my name… He knows my every thought… He sees each tear that falls and hears me when I call." Alex wondered who "He" was and if there was any chance that "He" knew Alex's name for sure. He peeked over the balcony, but he didn't see any men around anywhere. Who could this "He" be? God? At the same time he thought it, Alex wondered where that had come from. Suddenly, a man in long robes stepped through a door and walked onto what looked like a stage to Alex, at the front of the church. Maybe he was the "He" that those ladies were singing about. Maybe he would know Alex's name for sure.

The man spoke to the women for a few minutes and thanked them for coming. After that he bowed his head and said, "Let us pray."

Now Alex had heard those words before. He felt all warm and fuzzy inside, as if this had been a good experience for him. He felt like he knew about God and everything, but it just wasn't completely clear in his head. Nothing from the past seemed clear to Alex. He always had these little flashes of thoughts and memories and feelings, but he couldn't make them stay or come into focus for very long. Alex sighed and listened to the man praying. Did God really hear prayers, he wondered. Did he really do so many things that people should be thankful for? Did he know who Alex was and what had happened to him? Alex rubbed the back of his head, still able to feel the rough bump and scab. He remembered waking up in the dump and the bag and the rat and the stink and the horror he had felt at first. He didn't think that God could know who he was. Someone that important would not let bad things happen. But then he thought about yesterday and Mr. Thompson and the shoes and food. Maybe Alex should try to find out how to get to know this God better. He rubbed at his forehead. The headache was coming back. Alex had to get out of here. It suddenly seemed way too loud and stuffy. He crept back to the last flight of stairs and on down to the hallway that led to the door outside. No one in sight! Alex tiptoed down the hallway, quietly opened and closed the door, and escaped.

8

THE JOB

On Saturday morning Alex woke up early, filled with excited jitters. He started to jump out of bed in anticipation and whacked his head hard on the low ceiling. In his excitement to go back to Mr. Thompson's store, he had forgotten about the low roof over his head. Rubbing his head gently, he crawled off the rickety cot, straightened the blankets, and fumbled his way out of the storage room. He quickly made his way down from the bell tower, always watchful and quiet, and hurried to the restroom on the lower level of the church. Alex rarely used the restrooms on the main level for fear of being discovered. This bathroom was much smaller, but it had a lock on the door, and Alex knew he would not be disturbed. He used the toilet and washed his hands quickly. The night before Alex had made a valiant attempt to clean up. He stared at himself in the tiny, clouded mirror on the wall over the sink. He desperately needed a haircut! Maybe he would ask Mr. Thompson about a barber where he could get a haircut. He didn't want Mr. Thompson to think that he liked looking this way.

Alex used the little bar of soap on the sink to wash his face and arms again. He dried them on the rough paper towels. It was not much of an improvement, considering his filthy clothes, but it was the best he could do today. Alex hurried back upstairs to get something to eat. He had no idea how long he would be gone today, but he was going to be prepared. He decided to eat the apple he had purchased yesterday at the convenience store, a few blocks away. Alex hated going in there because it was not very clean and the men who worked there scared him. But yesterday, as he was hurrying down the street, he saw the apple through the window and was tempted! He had some of the money from the pouch in his pocket, so he had gathered his courage, gone in the store, and bought the apple. The man behind the counter had been busy on the phone and had not even looked twice at Alex. The apple had cost sixty-nine cents, which had seemed like a lot of money to Alex. However, munching on the apple this morning, Alex thought it was worth it after all.

Alex finished the apple and put together a quick sandwich of bread and cheese. He wrapped the sandwich in a clean piece of cloth and looked around for something to carry it in. He spied the wrinkled brown sack of batteries on the shelf. He dumped the batteries into an old, empty box and carefully placed his sandwich in the paper sack. He was ready to go. Alex put his things out of sight under the crate and looked around to make sure everything was in its place. He didn't want to leave any signs of living here if he could help it. He left the bell tower and quietly shut the door. He was on his way to his first job.

Alex made it safely to the store, constantly looking over his shoulder for the gang of boys who had chased him. He knew it was almost nine o'clock because he had looked at the clock in the back of the church on his way out. He wanted to be at the store as early as possible, so he didn't dawdle. He was thinking that he might be able to earn some clean clothes today if he did a good job at the store. He hoped that Mr. Thompson had something that would fit him. Right now he thought that just about anything would be better than what he was wearing.

Mr. Thompson was already in the store sorting through a large box of clothing when Alex walked up to the front door. He waved at Alex to come in. "I wasn't sure if you would show up today, young fella," Mr. Thompson said as Alex walked up. "I sure can use your help!" He smiled at Alex and noticed the wrinkled sack clutched in his nervous hands, and the socks and shoes on his feet that looked so much better than the old ragged shoes. "Put your lunch in the back room, and I'll get you started."

Alex hurried back to the small room where Mr. Thompson had given him cookies earlier in the week. He put his sandwich in the old refrigerator and wiped his sweaty hands on his pants. Then he returned to the front of the store anxiously.

Mr. Thompson showed Alex how to sort out the good usable clothing from the clothing that would just be torn up and used as rags. He explained that he would like to get all the windows washed today if possible and that they could use the rags in the process. He showed Alex how to take the ragged clothes and tear or cut them into squares to be used for washing windows. Alex worked hard taking the clothes from the rag pile and using the heavy scissors that Mr. Thompson handed him to cut the old shirts, pants, and towels into squares (well, almost squares) and stack them in a pile to be used to clean windows. He picked up a red T-shirt that was old and faded, but obviously cleaner than what he had on, and longingly thought about switching it with what he was wearing. Mr. Thompson, noticing the look, nonchalantly told Alex that he might want to keep out a shirt or two that would be a little cooler for washing windows. Alex looked up startled, to see if he was serious, but Mr. Thompson was busy digging down in the box of clothes for more. He quickly undid the buttons of his long-sleeved shirt, slipped it off, and tugged on the clean T-shirt. It felt wonderful! He picked out another faded blue T-shirt from the pile and folded it carefully. "I'll just run these to the back room," he said as he wadded up his dirty shirt and taking the folded T-shirt scurried out of sight.

Mr. Thompson shook his head and smiled and wondered where this child had come from. Alex hurried back and got to work. Before long Alex had a tall pile of rags beside him. Mr. Thompson told him he had plenty of rags to get started on the windows. He showed Alex where to get hot water and soap and handed him a large, plastic bucket. Alex was ready to go to work! He went back to the big sink in a little washroom next to the break room and started filling up the bucket. As he waited, he looked around and noticed a curtain in the corner. Alex couldn't help himself. He looked over his shoulder quickly then cautiously took a peek behind the curtain. A shower! Behind the plastic lined curtain was a dingy, tin shower. Alex thought longingly of a clean, hot spray of water washing away the grime on his hair and body. He suddenly had a brand new reason for working hard today!

Alex scrubbed windows tirelessly all morning, happily day dreaming about hot water and how it would feel to be clean at last. He wondered how he would approach Mr. Thompson about being allowed to use the shower, what he would do for a towel (although at this point he was willing to drip dry!), and the possibility of earning some of the clean clothing he had sorted earlier. He had spotted a pair of pants that he thought would fit him along with the other clean T-shirt he had put back. He had even noticed some decent-looking underwear, if he could only be brave enough to mention it. He might have to forget about that though. It would be too embarrassing. Still, clean pants and a shirt would be a huge improvement over what he had.

Mr. Thompson noticed Alex. He noticed his excitement with the new shirt. He noticed how hard Alex worked at making the windows shine. He noticed his daydreaming. While Alex worked, Mr. Thompson continued to sort clothing. Unknown to Alex, however, he was quietly making a pile of things that he thought might fit the boy. Pants, shirts, underwear, and pajamas went into the pile. That boy needed some clothes! Mr. Thompson didn't have a clue as to how he would get Alex to take the things, but he would worry about that later. He piled them all into a big bag and set them off to the side. He would find a way.

In the meantime, Alex had finished the windows. He was dirty and smudged from head to toe, but the windows were sparkling. He hurried over to Mr. Thompson and sat down the bucket of dirty water. "I'm finished," he told Mr. Thompson. Mr. Thompson walked over to take a look at the windows. He scowled a little. He walked over to the other side of the building to look at the windows there. He scratched his whiskery chin. "Now how did you manage to get all of those filthy windows so clean?" he wondered out loud. Then he looked directly at Alex and smiled. "It looks like all the dirt jumped right off the windows and on to you!" he exclaimed. "You're a real mess!"

Alex looked down at his dirty clothes, obviously upset. "Don't you worry about it, Alex. I have a shower here and you can wash it all right down the drain! You just grab that bag of clothes over there and head right back to the room where you got the hot water. There's a shower in the corner, some towels in the cupboard under the sink and everything you should need to get all spiffed up. Go on now! Go get yourself cleaned up so you can eat your lunch. You can't eat all filthy like that." Mr. Thompson walked over and grabbed the bag of clothing that he had sorted out. "See if there isn't something in there that you can wear for now, boy. And take the rest of it home. If it doesn't fit you, give it to someone who can wear it. I have more clothes than I know what to do with."

Alex just stood there. This was unbelievable! He didn't even have to ask to use the shower. He was being told to use it! And he was being given clean clothes, maybe even underwear. Tears started in his eyes, but he blinked them away. He couldn't let Mr. Thompson know how much this meant to him. "Yes sir!" he mumbled. "I'll get a shower right away. Thanks for the stuff. I'll hurry!" He grabbed the bag and hurried toward the back of the store.

"Take your time," he heard Mr. Thompson reply. "You've earned it."

Shaking his head and chuckling to himself, Mr. Thompson stood looking out the front of the store. What young boy would be anxious to take a bath in this day and age? He just couldn't figure this boy out. Nope! He was going to have to keep him around for a while. And what would the missus say about this one? She'd be baking up a storm before next Saturday. She might even grace the old "dump" with her presence before long. Yes, she might at that!

Alex quickly shut the door to the water room and scurried to get what he needed. He grabbed a big, old towel from the cabinet under the sink and hurried over to the shower. He pulled back the dingy, plastic curtain and quickly turned on the hot water faucet. Warm water sprayed out making a "tinny" noise against the walls. The water started getting hotter, so Alex added a bit of cold and quickly stripped off his filthy clothing. He scrambled into the shower and almost cried at the wonderful feeling of hot water rushing over his body. He reached up and grabbed some soap and started lathering every inch of his body. Oh what a feeling! Feeling guilty and a little nervous, Alex put the soap back and picked up a bottle of shampoo. He quickly poured a small amount in his hand and rubbed it into his hair. Placing the shampoo back in the shower caddy, he scrubbed his head till it tingled, careful of the spot at the base of his skull. He rinsed the last bit of shampoo and soap from his hair and body and reluctantly shut off the water. He stepped out of the shower a grabbed the big towel. It felt so good to be clean!

Alex dried off and searched quickly through the bag for underwear, socks, and a pair of pants. Everything he found fit him better than what he had on. The jeans he found in the bag were well worn but clean and without holes. There were socks and a couple of shirts, two more pairs of pants, and assorted underwear. There was even a pair of cotton pajamas! Alex pulled on underwear, socks, and the jeans and the faded blue T-shirt that felt soft from being washed many times. He stuffed the rest of the clothing back into the bag and reached for his shoes. It felt so wonderful to have so many clean things to wear. He felt like singing for joy. He carefully tucked the shower curtain back over the shower and made sure the water was turned off tight. He carried his old clothing to the trashcan in the corner and dumped it in! Wow! Those clothes smelled HORRIBLE! He never wanted to touch them again. He opened the door and carried the bag to the snack room to leave it with his other things. There sat Mr. Thompson, with a big smile on his face, waiting for Alex to have lunch.

"Well look at you!" Mr. Thompson exclaimed. "There really is a boy under all that grime. You clean up pretty nicely, kid."

Alex looked sheepishly at Mr. Thompson. "Thank you, sir." He sat the bag in the corner and moved quickly to the refrigerator to get his lunch. He grabbed the brown bag and hurried to the table to join Mr. Thompson. Alex took out his sandwich and laid it on a napkin that he had hesitantly taken from a pile on the table. Mr. Thompson watched him silently, then suddenly folded his hands over his own sandwich and bowed his head. Alex knew that he was praying. He quickly bowed his own head and watched out of the corner of his eye to see Mr. Thompson murmuring words to himself. Without thinking, he squeezed his eyes shut and started mouthing something that came to him from nowhere. "Bless this food we are about to enjoy and the hands that prepared it. Amen." Alex looked up startled, wondering where in the world those words had come from. He noticed that Mr. Thompson was watching him as he ate his sandwich.

Alex quickly unwrapped his sandwich and bit into it. Boy it tasted good! He had worked up an appetite. Mr. Thompson helped himself to a cookie from the container on the table and passed the container over to Alex. "You better help me eat these, kid. Mrs. Thompson will be upset if I don't bring home an empty container tonight, now that she knows I have someone working for me. She'll be baking up a storm this weekend. And don't be surprised if she shows up to take a look at you. She's the mothering type, my Irene. Yes she is. And once she gets a look at you, she'll be trying to fatten you up."

Alex took a cookie nervously. "Thank you, Mr. Thompson. What would you like me to do next?"

Alex worked all afternoon for Mr. Thompson. He swept the floor with an old broom that he got from the washroom, feeling especially lighthearted and thankful after the hot shower and lunch. He worked carefully, moving tables to sweep underneath and in the corners. When he was finished, he helped Mr. Thompson carry some of the bags and boxes from the storeroom. They sorted out the good items of clothing, toys, and household goods and stacked them on the shelves and tables. Mr. Thompson used an old sticker gun to put prices on everything and directed Alex as to where he wanted the different items. Before long, Alex knew where things belonged. They worked in silence for the most part, with Mr. Thompson waiting on an occasional customer from time to time.

Mr. Thompson had watched Alex working quietly all afternoon. He was amazed at how the boy stayed on task. He wondered again about his family and background. It was obvious that there were problems, yet the boy was so pleasant to have around. Mr. Thompson had noticed Alex's reluctance to comment about personal issues. He was afraid to scare him off with too many questions. The boy obviously appreciated coming to the store, and all that had happened so far. He looked like a different child today, since he had cleaned up. He almost seemed normal. Patience, he thought. He hoped the boy would keep coming back until he could figure it all out. Well, enough for today. It was time to close up shop.

At five minutes to four, Mr. Thompson called Alex over to the cash register. "It's time to close for today, Alex," he said. "Now how much do I owe you, son?" Mr. Thompson scratched his whiskery chin and thought for a moment. "Let's see," he said. "You worked three and a half hours this morning and three hours this afternoon. What do you say to about two dollars per hour?"

Alex looked at Mr. Thompson in amazement, almost horror. "M-Mr. Thompson, s-sir, you don't have to pay me," Alex stammered. "I was working for the clothes and the shower." Alex quickly ran back to the lunch room and grabbed the bag of clothing. "This is enough, really sir," he said in a hurry.

"Nonsense!" replied Mr. Thompson. "You worked hard all day. I don't expect you to do that without getting paid. Those clothes are a fringe benefit of working here. Do you know what a fringe benefit is, son?"

Alex was embarrassed. "N-No, sir," he answered.

"Well, a fringe benefit is when you get something extra as part of the agreement for working in a place of business. You work in a restaurant, you get to eat a certain amount for free. You work at a garage, you might get some free car service. You work in a place like this, you get to pick out certain things you need *without* paying for them. Do you understand now?" Alex nodded tentatively. Mr. Thompson opened the cash register and counted out thirteen dollars. "Here you go, son, I appreciate the hard work you did today. Now go on home and get yourself some supper. Mrs. Thompson and I have an appointment at five and she'll skin me alive if I'm late getting home."

"Thanks a lot, sir," Alex said, stuffing the money in his new jeans' pocket. "Would you like me to come back sometime?" he said anxiously.

Mr. Thompson scratched his chin again. "Well, son, I am supposed to get another truckload of stuff on Monday. Are you interested in moving another mountain?" He chuckled a little.

"Yes sir!" Alex replied (without a bit of nervousness, Mr. Thompson noticed). "That would be great! I'll get here by nine o'clock, sir!"

Mr. Thompson couldn't help but notice the anticipation on the boy's face. "You can also plan on every Saturday, if you're available," added Mr. Thompson. "I can always use help then."

"Okay, Mr. Thompson that would be great. I can do that." Alex started backing toward the door, carrying the bag of clothing. "Thank you for the clothes and stuff," he said as he continued toward the door. "I'll see you on Monday then."

"Okeydoke! See you, kid. Have a good weekend, and Alex?"

Alex turned around as he finally reached the door. "Yes sir?" he questioned.

"Try to get to church tomorrow, Alex."

"O-Okay, Mr. Thompson, I will. Thanks again!" Alex turned and almost ran down the street.

9

MEMORIES

Alex spent the rest of the day at "home" in the bell tower, folding his "new" clothing and stacking it in a couple of empty boxes he had pulled out of the jumble of cots and toys in his "room." The boxes had lids, so he carefully sorted the pajamas and underwear into one box and the shirts and jeans into another. He put the lids on the boxes and stacked them neatly at the end of his cot. As he was noticing that the boxes were about the same level as the cot and would support his feet where they hung over, a thought flashed into his brain! He saw a glimpse of the woman again! She was piling up boxes and marking on them with a big, black marker. Alex was helping her, and she looked at him sadly. She seemed to be saying she was sorry. Alex tried to tell her it was okay, but she just smiled sadly and faded away. Alex sat down sharply on the floor. He was stunned and confused. Who *was* this lady? He thought it might be the same lady who screamed his name in his nightmares, and he was pretty sure it was the same one who had flashed into his mind when he was eating the cookie at Mr. Thompson's store. Was this lady his mom? Where was she?

Alex shook off the spooky feeling. Nothing made any sense at all. His stomach was growling, and he realized that it would be getting dark soon. He thought about the Corner Café and decided it was time for another hot meal. He had thirteen dollars in his pocket and wouldn't even have to use any of money in the pouch that was stashed in the battery box of an old, dilapidated teddy bear under his cot. And today he even felt clean! Other than needing a haircut, he felt like he was looking pretty good. He carefully closed the door and made his way outside.

Alex walked quickly to the Corner Café. He opened the door and immediately noticed the waitress who had waited on him the last time. She was carrying a huge plate of food to a customer at a table in the corner. He quickly sat down at the same table he had used before. When the waitress turned around, she looked at him and smiled hesitantly. "Hello there, do I know you?" she asked.

"I-I came here for soup a couple of nights ago," Alex stammered.

"Oh yes, I remember now." The waitress acted like she didn't really know what he was talking about. "Do you know what you want to order?"

Alex grabbed the menu from the center of the table. "Um…a glass of milk and…and…" He scanned the menu quickly, looking at what seemed like hundreds of items to him.

"Tell you what," said the waitress, "I'll bring the milk while you decide. My name is Carol. I'll be right back to take your order."

Alex stared at her as she walked away. He felt like such a dummy! While Carol was getting his milk, Alex decided on a bowl of vegetable beef stew for supper. Carol walked away wondering in disbelief if this could be the same dirty, ragged-looking boy she had worried about on Wednesday night. She thought about the bag of good used clothing she had brought in the next day, hoping that he would come back. Should she offer him the clothing? He sure looked a lot cleaner today. Still, he had such a lost look about him. She'd have to think of something while he was eating.

Carol returned to the table with Alex's milk. He ordered a bowl of vegetable beef stew. "That comes with a muffin," she told him. "Would you like blueberry, banana-nut, or a corn muffin?"

"A corn muffin will be fine," Alex replied politely.

Carol had a sudden idea. "You know, my brother's favorite muffin is a corn muffin. You kind of remind me of him."

Alex didn't really know what to say as Carol walked away to get his stew. Maybe that was why she kept looking at him so funny. He took a sip of his milk. A few minutes later, the waitress brought his stew and muffin, and as another customer called for her attention, Alex looked in amazement at the huge bowl of stew and the *two* large corn muffins sitting side by side, along with butter in a little paper cup. He was really hungry by now, but as he picked up his spoon, a sudden image of the lady in his dreams bowing her head over a meal with her hand reaching out for his made Alex stop short of digging in. Without realizing what he was doing or why, Alex bowed his head and repeated the prayer that had come into his thoughts at Mr. Thompson's store: "Thank you, Lord, for this food and for the hands that prepared it. Amen." Suddenly Alex felt better. He felt like someone was watching over him. Maybe it *was* God. He dug into his stew and muffin with relish.

As Carol waited on other customers in the restaurant, a plan began to form in her mind. She watched Alex devour his food as she went about her job, and when she saw he was almost done, she stopped at his table. "Will there be anything else for you tonight, young man?" she asked.

"No thank you," he replied.

"Okay, I'll get your check then. Would you like a bag for that extra muffin?"

"Yes please," Alex replied politely. He finished up the last bite of stew as Carol went to get his bill.

Carol brought his check and laid it on his table. "Thanks. Come back and see us soon. Oh, by the way, do you know of any churches in the area? My mom asked me to drop off a couple of bags of stuff that my little brother doesn't want, and she said there was a church near the café. You don't know where it is, do you?"

Alex looked a little startled at first, and then quickly answered Carol. "Yeah, there's one just a couple of blocks away. I know right where it is. Would you like me to drop the stuff off for you?"

"Oh, could you?" Carol replied. "That would be great, and I think you can manage the bags if it isn't too far. Let me get them." She hurried off to get the things that she had brought in for Alex, smiling to herself.

Now Carol had no idea that the church nearby was where Alex lived, since she had her own plans in mind. As she returned with two large shopping bags of stuff that she thought Alex could use, she planned what she would say. She sat the two bags down next to Alex's table. "There's a lot of stuff in here," she said, "but my brother doesn't want any of it. He's the baby you know. Some of these things have never even been used. Feel free to go through it all before you drop it off. Maybe there's something you would like yourself. Whatever you don't want you can drop off at the church. How's that? But don't feel like you have to keep any of it." Carol picked up Alex's check and money and walked over to the cash register while Alex stared at the two large bags of clothing, books, and stuff. When she returned with his change, she laid it on the table and thanked Alex again.

"I really appreciate you doing this and saving me a trip. I hope you can use some of it. Come in again. I always work on Mondays and Wednesdays and Saturdays. Just ask for me if you come back! See you!"

Alex stammered good-bye as Carol dashed off to take another order. He looked at the two bags in disbelief. What was all this stuff? Was there anything he could use? Suddenly excited about what might be in the bags, he picked up his change and quickly counted out the correct tip. He stuffed his extra muffin in the bag that Carol had left on the table and placed it carefully into one of the large bags as he stood up. Grabbing the handles of a bag with each hand, he awkwardly left the café. The bags were heavy, and Alex was worried a bit about getting them to the church. He never even noticed Carol smiling at him over the top of a booth as he left the café. As Alex drew close to the church, he had another sudden flash of memory. He was walking with the lady in his dreams and they were carrying big shopping bags. The snow was falling gently down and the lady was laughing at Alex, because as small as he was, he was trying to carry the largest bags. A brief feeling of intense love and happiness washed over Alex, but it was gone as quick as it had come. A heavy cloud of despair settled on his shoulders as he reached the church and trudged upstairs with his heavy load. He had to stop at the top of each flight of stairs to catch his breath, but he finally made it safely to the bell tower. He was worn out from his eventful day, so he fished out his “new” pajamas and decided to call it a night.

10

CHURCH AND STUFF

Sunday morning dawned, bright and early, with sunshine streaming through the side windows of the bell tower and the music of the chimes playing in the background. Alex listened to the chimes as they pealed out the invitation to come to church.

Alex had been unbelievably exhausted, both physically and mentally, by the time he had hauled the heavy bags up to his "home" in the church. He had fallen across his cot after peeling off his clothes and putting on his pajamas, feeling a desperate sense of loneliness and loss. Fortunately, he was so tired he had fallen asleep immediately and slept soundly the whole night through. As he lay there, Alex heard the sound of the organ music as it floated up through the air from the sanctuary below him. Suddenly, a picture of Mr. Thompson flashed briefly through his thoughts. He remembered the kindness that he had been shown and the remark Mr. Thompson had made about church. Alex had a sudden urge to please Mr. Thompson in return for all he had done for him. He knew he could tell Mr. Thompson that he was "in church" on Sunday and not be lying, but today he just wanted to really be part of "going to church." Besides, he thought to himself, who would even notice one small, quiet boy sitting in the crowd. He could slip into the back row without much difficulty.

Alex jumped up and scurried around the bell tower getting ready. He pulled out a clean pair of pants that Mr. Thompson had given him and selected the nicest shirt. Quickly he changed into the fresh clothing and pulled on clean socks and shoes. It felt wonderful to have a change of clothing! He hurried downstairs to use the bathroom and brush his teeth with the brand new toothbrush and toothpaste that he had purchased at the convenience store on his way home the day before. His step was a little bit lighter as he stuffed the toothbrush in his pocket and headed out toward the main church building.

Stealthily, Alex made his way down the main hall and into the sanctuary area. He stood in the very back of the church, near the staircase going up to the balcony and eventually to the bell tower. He could hear the whole congregation singing to the tune of the organ music. Feeling a little anxious, Alex slipped into an empty spot near the back behind a family of four. He grabbed a hymnal and opened it up like he was singing. Inwardly, he felt like shouting for joy! He was in church! Mr. Thompson was going to be so proud! Before he could get that thought out of his head, Alex surprised himself for the second time in moments. He started singing the song! He actually knew the words! Before he knew what he was doing, Alex was singing, "You came from heaven to earth, to show the way, from the earth to the cross, my debt to pay! From the cross to the grave, from the grave to the sky, Lord I lift your name on high!" Now where on earth had that come from? As the congregation finished singing the song and waited to be seated, Alex sat down with a thump and wondered what was going on. He struggled as hard as he could to remember where he had heard that song before. Briefly a glimpse of a group of kids in a camp setting flitted through his mind, but he could not hold on to it.

As he shook his head to clear his thoughts, he realized that a big, white-haired gentleman was talking up front. Alex recognized him as a man he had seen before in the church. He started paying attention to what the man was saying. Matthew 7:1–5 tells us what Jesus had to say about judging others. He did not want us to judge others without mercy. In fact, it is not our job to judge people at all. He went on to tell a story about something that had happened to him at the grocery store. As his voice droned on, Alex started looking around at the people in the congregation. There were old people and young people and families. Alex saw a woman lean over to a child and whisper something in his ear. Suddenly tears welled up in his eyes and he started feeling choked up. Alex knew he was desperately missing his mother. He *must* have a mother somewhere. Where was she? Why had she left him all alone? Did he have a dad too, or siblings? Why didn't he remember? Why didn't he *know*? As the man up front announced the next song and everyone rose to sing again, Alex slipped out of the pew and headed out the door. He just couldn't do it! He couldn't sit there alone and see everyone else sitting together. He had no one who cared about him. He needed to get out quick and get some fresh air!

The bright sunshine outside lifted his spirits as soon as the door closed behind him. He quickly gulped in fresh air and started walking. It was time to get away for a bit and think of something else besides what he was missing. Alex reached in his pocket and felt for the money he had put in there this morning when he got ready. Five dollars and some change. It would do.

He must have walked for five or six blocks, trying to shut out the loneliness by thinking about the service and the fact that he could sing and how good it felt to be clean. He thought about God and a sort of peacefulness settled over him. Somehow he felt that God was with him and understood what he was feeling. It just felt right in his heart. He looked around the area for a sign of something familiar. He had headed in the opposite direction of Mr. Thompson's store, and it occurred to him that he hadn't really seen much of anything on this side of the church. He noticed it was a little cleaner in this direction and he was starting to see more activity. Traffic noise was louder now, and up ahead he spied the golden arches of a McDonald's. Alex realized, as his stomach growled loudly, that he hadn't eaten anything this morning. Did he dare to spend money on breakfast? *Oh, what the heck*, he thought, *it's Sunday, and tomorrow I'm going back to help Mr. Thompson again! I can afford a little breakfast!* His step lightened as he hurried toward the sign. When he reached McDonald's, he quickly went inside. He stepped up to the counter and looked at his choices. He ordered a pancake breakfast, paid quietly, and found a table in a corner by the window.

He sat down to eat, saying a quick prayer without even consciously realizing what he was doing. He gazed out the window, not really registering what was going on. He watched people and traffic go by, marveling at the variety of both. A few blocks down the road that ran along this side of McDonald's, he noticed a sign that looked like a grocery store of some kind, and further down a ways what looked like a red-and-white barber pole. Hey! Maybe he could get a haircut! It was worth checking out. As he finished eating, he remembered the bags he had dragged upstairs last night. Suddenly he felt a little better. He had a warm breakfast in his tummy, money in his pocket, and two large bags of "stuff" to discover. He decided he would go back to his room and look through the bags. Then he would get a bit more cash and check out the grocery store. If he had time, he would see if there really was a barbershop where he could get a haircut. In a much happier frame of mind, he finished the last bite of pancakes, washed it down with the rest of his milk, and gathered up his trash. He dropped it off in the waste container and hurried out the door. He made his way back to the church, down the hallway, and slipped upstairs without being noticed. He entered the bell room and pulled the large bags out into the middle of the room.

The first bag was mostly filled with clothing. Right on top was a navy blue jacket with red trim and fuzzy gray lining. Alex knew it would come in handy. He slipped it on and found that it couldn't have fit better if it had been made for him. Next in the bag was a pair of dark gray, corduroy pants and a pair of jeans that had not been worn. The tags were still attached! Alex held them up and knew they would fit. They might be a little bit long, but he'd make them work. There was a matching sweater in the same gray with red-and-black stripes, and also a button-down shirt in charcoal-and-red plaid. Alex felt like Christmas had come early! Did he dare to keep this stuff?

As he went on, he came across a school uniform, baseball pants, and a lime green sweat shirt. Alex knew that he would not use those items, so he piled them to one side to put back in the bag. Next he pulled out a soft, thick flannel shirt, several pairs of striped boxer shorts, and a package of socks (three pairs!) that had never even been opened.

Alex almost cried for the second time that day! He carried all of the new clothing (and most of it was *literally* new!) over to the cot and stacked it there. He went back and packed the things he didn't want or need back into the bag and set it aside. Eagerly he reached for the second bag. On top was a small, cuddly fleece blanket that Alex thought would come in handy as the weather turned cooler. Under that was a pair of sturdy, black shoes. Eagerly Alex pulled them out and held them up to his feet. They would fit him, he knew they would! Quickly he took off a sneaker and stepped into a shoe. They were only a little bit too large. With some thick socks, they would be just fine. Alex could not believe his luck. They were almost new! He took off the shoe and carefully placed them under his cot. In his excitement to see what else was in the bag, he didn't even put his sneaker back on! Next were some school supplies, including a couple of spiral notebooks and a pouch with pencils, pens, scissors, and tape. Alex set them aside sadly. He wanted to go to school, but how could he? He shook off the feeling and reached back into the bag. A couple of CDs were next and a couple of paperback books. Alex placed them in the bag with the things he couldn't use. At the very bottom of the bag was a thick leather-bound book. As Alex pulled it out, he realized immediately that it was a Bible. The words "Holy Bible" embossed on the cover reinforced the thought. The Bible felt comfortable in Alex's hands. He wanted it. For some reason, it just felt familiar.

Alex knew that he was keeping a lot of the stuff that Carol had asked him to bring to the church, but he also knew that he needed it. He had no idea when he would be able to wash any of his clothes. He knew that eventually he would have to find a way, but at least he had some extra things to wear in the meantime. Alex placed everything he was keeping in the second bag. He went to his cot and reached for the dilapidated bear underneath it. He unzipped the battery pouch and pulled out his carefully folded money. He pulled off the twenty dollar bill, replaced the rest back in the bear, and stuffed it back into its hiding place. He gathered the bag of leftover things and carried them down to main level of the church. Next to the entryway, there was a large box marked "DONATIONS." He placed the bag in the box and headed outside.

11

TROUBLE

Happily Alex started back in the direction he had gone that morning. He saw the golden arches again and headed toward the barber's pole. He noticed the sign for the grocery store and looked in the window as he passed. It wasn't huge, but it would certainly have some things that Alex could use. Right now, Alex wanted a haircut! He went another block and turned in the direction of what he was sure was a barbershop. As he rounded the corner, disappointment stared him in the face. It wasn't a barbershop—it was an *old* barbershop that had been turned into a used appliance store. Television sets filled the window in every direction, with different programs on every other set. The result was a cacophony of sounds and pictures accompanied by an overwhelming sense of chaos. Alex trudged on. Why did days have the ability to go sour so quickly?

As he trudged on, he thought about the service this morning. The momentary joy he had felt while singing suddenly flitted into his head. His step lightened a little, and he started to put things into perspective. It wasn't the worst thing he had to deal with. There must be a barbershop somewhere around here. Besides, he would be seeing Mr. Thompson tomorrow. Maybe he would get an opportunity to ask him about a barbershop. He thought about the new belongings he had discovered back at the church. He really had a lot to be thankful for today. Yeah, he did.

It had to be somewhere around two o'clock or so, and after having a late breakfast that morning, he wasn't hungry yet, or ready to go back to the church. He knew he had time to spare before returning to the grocery store. He passed a woman holding the hand of a small child and kept on going. He started thinking about the service that morning and wondering about the lady in his dreams. Would he ever know who she was?

Many blocks later, Alex suddenly realized he had traveled farther than he intended, and without paying much attention to where he was going. He looked around him and could see that he was heading into a rough, less populated area without much traffic. Suddenly, from a run-down building across the street, two of the boys from the gang who had chased him came shuffling out, with cigarettes dangling from their mouths. One of them glanced up and saw Alex. With a whoop, he was across the street, with the second boy close behind. With a sharp punch in the stomach, he had knocked Alex to the ground before he knew what hit him. Before Alex could even catch his breath, the other boy had him by the hair. Struggling to get to his hands and knees, with one boy jerking him by the hair and the other kicking him in rapid succession, Alex knew he was in trouble. A vicious kick to his head and he felt the blood running down his face. He fell flat on his face, chin first on the uneven sidewalk, and each of the boys grabbed a leg and started dragging him across the street toward the abandoned building.

Alex had to struggle to keep from passing out. His already pounding head was bumping and banging along the ground. His body hurt everywhere, and he felt like he was going to vomit. They made it across the street and dumped him in a dark corner of the building with a thud. One of the boys pulled a dirty kerchief out of his pocket and quickly began tying Alex's hands behind his back. Alex tried to think clearly and keep his hands as far apart as possible without being obvious. The other boy was grinning at Alex and making crude comments to him about making him his slave. Coming closer to Alex, he dangled a frayed piece of rope in front of him. After slapping Alex across the face with it a couple of times, he bent over to wrap it around Alex's ankles and tie it as tight as possible. Alex felt the welts rising on his face as cold sweat trickled down his back. The two boys stood up and looked at Alex in satisfaction. "So Raggedy Andy, what do you have to say for yourself?" Alex glared back at them, refusing to say a word. Suddenly, they all heard a police siren coming closer. The two boys looked at each other and ran to the doorway. After a few mumbled words, they took off running. Alex just sat there, stunned. Without warning, his vision began to blur and he slumped to the ground.

When Alex came to, he could barely make out the door opening to the outside. He knew it must be getting dark. How long had he been lying there? He tried to sit up and realized that his hands and feet were tied. Everything came rushing back. His head ached so badly that he could hardly think. Before he could get his wits about him, he heard a rustling sound close by. He struggled with his hands but could not get them unbound. He looked across the building and thought he saw a shadow moving. Yes! It was something moving toward him. Was it an animal? It seemed to be crawling directly toward him. Alex tried to scoot himself up against the wall, but his feet were numb and would not support him. He cringed as he watched the shadow coming closer and closer. Was it a dog? It seemed to be walking on four legs. The hair stood out on Alex's arms and legs, and the sweat started dribbling down his back again. Wait a minute! It wasn't a dog, it was a small boy! He appeared to be crawling along slowly, but Alex's vision was so blurry he couldn't be sure. He blinked rapidly, trying hard to clear his eyes. When the boy got near him, Alex scooted further into the corner, trying to avoid him. What was he going to do?

As the boy stopped in front of Alex, he noticed that he looked much older than his size warranted and was in fact a wizened old man. He stared at Alex blankly, but he pushed at Alex trying to get behind him. At first Alex resisted, but besides being too weak to struggle, he suddenly realized that the man was trying to get to his hands to untie them. When the thought finally made it through the pounding in his head, Alex managed to slump to one side to give him access to his bound hands. Quickly, the scruffy little man went to work, although Alex felt nothing. His hands must have gone to sleep. After a few minutes the man returned with the kerchief that had been tied around his wrists, and Alex realized that his hands were free. He kept glancing toward the door, petrified that the other boys would come back. Thank God that Jake and Redman had not been with them. But maybe they would all come back! Panic flooded his brain! The man was watching too, and at a sudden banging noise, he started to dart away from Alex. However, they both heard an engine start revving and they realized that somewhere nearby people had gotten into a vehicle and started it up. After another long minute or two, they watched a dilapidated old pickup truck rambling by the open door. The little man was back in a flash working on Alex's feet. Finally, Alex felt the rope come loose and pulled his feet free from the rope. He tried to get to his feet, but his legs were numb and his arms felt like soggy noodles. The little man shook his head and pushed Alex back down.

The enormity of the whole situation came crashing down on his shoulders!

Alex was afraid! What had he gotten himself into? Who was this little man with the wizened, old face? Alex rubbed at his arms and legs trying to get the circulation going again. Before he could even begin to figure out what was happening, he heard the boys from the gang coming back. They were laughing loudly and talking crudely about the "stupid cops." Panic spread across Alex's face as he tried once more to stand.

He fell quickly to his knees, almost on top of the small man. The man tugged at Alex's clothing and motioned him to follow. He scuttled back the way he had come, with Alex crawling right on his heels. They traveled through a doorway on the far side of the room, and Alex found himself crawling on his hands and knees through a dark, narrow hallway. The ceiling was partially caved in, and there was water and debris everywhere. Alex was amazed at how quickly the little man traveled. His own hands and knees were already aching from the rough surface, but he was determined to keep up. There was no way he was going to let those boys get their hands on him again!

Alex could hear the boys fumbling around and cursing in the room behind him as they realized he was gone. He prayed that they couldn't see him in the dark, but he broke out in a cold sweat just hearing their voices. Suddenly, the small boy just dropped out of sight in front of Alex! Before he could even blink, he felt himself falling. With a sharp thump, he hit bottom and lay stunned in the darkness. As his eyes grew accustomed to the darkness, he saw the man sitting beside him with a huge, strange grin on his face. They had landed on an old mattress that had been dragged directly beneath the hole in the hallway. Once again, the man motioned to Alex to follow him. He stood up shakily and followed the man, who walked in a jerky hop. They wound their way through a maze of rubble and old belongings, until Alex could see a dim light up ahead. As they drew closer, he realized there was a small opening between two walls, where the evening light was filtering through. As he followed the man outside, he could tell that they had come out the opposite side of the house, on the lower level. Alex was never so glad to be outside in his life!

As quickly as the man had come, he was gone! Alex was so startled he just stood there blinking. Had he imagined him? Tears started in his eyes as he turned and headed as quickly as he could manage up a steep incline and back to street level. It was full dark by now and Alex was grateful. The darkness would hide him from the boys and anyone else. Alex made his way back in the direction that he hoped led toward the church, holding his side and crouching behind bushes. He stayed close to buildings where he would be hidden in the shadows. He watched over his shoulder constantly in fear of running into anyone. Tears ran shamelessly down his face as he thought about how close he had come to utter disaster and how much pain he felt. His head still ached and he had bumps and bruises everywhere. It seemed like an eternity before the outline of the church came into view.

God heard her prayers…prayers for safety for her son… prayers for strength and guidance…prayers for hope. He strengthened her faith and her determination as He guided him to safety.

12

MRS. THOMPSON AND DR. DAVID

Alex had crept silently up the stairs to the bell tower the night before, feeling sure that someone would grab him at any moment, and barely making it through the door and onto the cot before he had passed out in pain and exhaustion. He was afraid to know how much damage had been done, or what he looked like. As he woke to the light in the bell tower, he knew it was bad. He could feel the dried blood on his face and see the dirt and blood on his clothing. His head and chin ached, and when he gingerly reached his hand up to his chin, it was still oozing blood. One side of his body was so stiff it was hard to imagine walking. Still he hobbled out of bed and tried to walk toward the door. He cringed in pain and held on to his side as he contemplated his choices. He decided at the very least he was going to have to wash up and change clothing if he was going to try to make it to Mr. Thompson's store. Painstakingly, he unbuttoned his shirt and slipped it off his shoulders. He let it fall where it landed by his feet. He picked up a shirt that was folded over a box from a couple of days before and gingerly slipped his arms into it, one by one. Slowly, with tears running down his face in spite of himself, he buttoned the shirt. The whole process seemed to take an eternity, and Alex decided he would just have to wear the dirty jeans he had on. He couldn't bear the thought of tugging them off and finding clean ones to put on. He stood catching his breath and trying not to think about all of the steps he had to conquer before he reached the bathroom downstairs. He took a piece of cloth he had been using for a washcloth. He wanted to be ready to head outside the minute he got cleaned up a bit. He knew he would never make it back up the stairs and down again. It was still early, but by the time he hobbled all the way to Mr. Thompson's store, it should be open. Maybe he could ask to take another shower, if he could stay on his feet long enough to get some work done.

By the time Alex got cleaned up as best he could, his head was throbbing and his chin was trickling blood again. Stubbornly Alex started the trek to the store. Anxiously he watched for the gang, staying behind bushes and buildings whenever he could. Sweat rolled steadily down his back, but he continued putting one foot in front of the other. After about fifteen minutes he started wondering if he could make it to the store. Holding his side tightly with one hand, he kept going. When the store finally came into sight in the distance, Alex knew he would not be doing much work. He was going to be lucky to make it to the store at all. Maybe Mr. Thompson would let him take a hot shower anyway and sit down for a bit before he headed home. Finally, Alex reached the steps and climbed up to turn the doorknob. It was locked! Alex almost sobbed out loud. Slowly, he sat down on the steps and leaned his head against the door. Of all days, Mr. Thompson must be running late today. Or maybe it was not nine o'clock yet. Alex thought he might just rest a moment. If Mr. Thompson didn't show up soon, he would have to begin to make his way back.

It seemed like he had barely closed his eyes when Mr. Thompson's old pickup truck pulled up in front of the store. Seeing Alex sitting on the steps had caused him to stop there instead of pulling around to the back of the store as he usually did. Another car pulled up directly behind him as he climbed out of the truck and walked toward Alex.

"What in the dickens happened to you?" was the first thing out of Mr. Thompson's mouth. Alex looked at him blankly, not having a clue what to say. Before he could make up an excuse, a lady walked up next to Mr. Thompson. She started to say something, but before the words were formed, a loud gasp escaped from her mouth and her hand flew up to stifle it. "Are you all right, son?" Mr. Thompson spoke again.

"Well of course he isn't!" Mrs. Thompson said as she knelt toward Alex. "Would you be all right if you looked like that? Alex, isn't it, what happened to you?"

By now Alex had had a few moments to figure out that this must be *Mrs.* Thompson and to think up an excuse. "I-I fell," he stammered quickly, "but I'll be okay. I wanted to try to work today, but I'm not feeling well after all. I think I'll j-just rest awhile and head back home."

Mrs. Thompson was not having any of it. She had listened carefully to Alex, noting the split chin and the way he was holding his side. She hadn't missed the dirt and blood on his clothing either. Now that she was over the initial shock of seeing him, she was ready to take charge. Before Mr. Thompson could even form a reply, she stood up briskly and turned in his direction. "This young man will not be working today, Henry. Get him in my car. I'll take him over to see David and have him take a look at him. Then we'll decide what to do."

"Now, Tilly," Mr. Thompson started.

"Don't now Tilly me!" she snapped. "This boy needs a doctor."

Alex looked from one to the other in confusion. His head was beginning to fog over again from the pain. He couldn't even stutter out a protest. Before he knew what was happening, Mr. Thompson had scooped him up and headed for her car. Alex groaned in protest as his side was jiggled. He tried desperately to bear the pain, but the walk from the church had taken a toll. When Mr. Thompson reached for the seat belt and hooked it around his bruised body, the pain was too much and he blacked out again.

"Hurry up, Henry!" Mrs. Thompson demanded. "Do you think we should just take him to the hospital?"

Mr. Thompson quickly locked his truck and jumped into the car with Mrs. Thompson. "Scoot over, I'll drive," he said. "It's closer to David's office, let's go there first."

For once Mrs. Thompson didn't respond. She buckled her seat belt and prayed for Alex. All the way to her son's office, she kept looking over her shoulder at the small boy slumped in the backseat.

A few moments later, Mr. Thompson pulled into a small parking lot next to a red, brick building. He jumped out of the car and opened the rear door to get Alex. This time he gingerly unlatched the seat belt and lifted Alex from the car. Mrs. Thompson rushed ahead to open the door to the building and then rushed to find her son. David was guiding a mother with a tiny baby in her arms from his office. After saying good-bye, he turned and saw his parents. His smile of greeting turned to a look of concern as he spied Alex hanging limply in his father's arms. "He's been hurt pretty badly," his father commented.

"Bring him into my office," David said. "What happened to him?"

Mr. and Mrs. Thompson looked at each other. "He said he fell," they said in unison.

David looked at his parents and raised his eyebrows, then turned back to examine the boy. As he gently lifted Alex's head with one hand to lift his eyelids, he noticed the ragged, matted hair, with abrasions underneath. "Looks like he was dragged," he thought to himself. He lifted Alex's eyelids, noting the welts across his cheeks. As he tilted his chin to get a better look at the cut there, Alex began to stir. His eyes flickered and he made a motion to sit up. "Lie still there, youngster," David said quietly, "I want to help you." Alex's face was very pale and fear hovered in his eyes as he looked up at David. The doctor unbuttoned Alex's shirt and listened to his breathing. Gently he ran his hands along Alex's rib cage. Alex jerked when his hands were about halfway down one side. The doctor felt gingerly around the area then switched to the other side. The bruises stood out vividly on Alex's pale, thin body. Finally, he moved to a cabinet against the wall and took out a large roll of bandage. Very carefully, he wrapped the bandage around the small boy until it supported the area of pain. Next, he swabbed Alex's chin with some cleaning solution and squeezed it together gently with his fingers. "We're going to have to put in a couple of stitches here," he told Alex. "I'll be as quick and gentle as I can." He called a nurse over the intercom and asked her to come into his office to assist. Carefully he prepared the needle for stitches. In the meantime, the nurse gave Alex a shot to relax him and numb the area.

Mr. And Mrs. Thompson stood on the other side of the bed watching it all. At one moment, Alex turned their direction to avoid seeing the needle and noticed they were holding hands. David quickly and efficiently stitched up Alex's chin. Before he could worry further, it was over. David cut the thread and handed the needle to the nurse. "Thanks," he said, and she left the room. "Now young man," he continued as he helped Alex sit up, "I think that will help. You have a slight concussion, a couple of badly bruised ribs, and three stitches in your chin. You're going to need to take it easy for a couple of days and rest a lot. I'll give you something for pain, and you need to let me know if you feel sick or have blurry vision. Otherwise, everything should heal just fine in time. Can I call your parents or someone to come pick you up?"

"I don't-they're not-I can make it home okay...," Alex stammered.

Turning to his parents, David's eyebrows rose once more. "Can I talk to you outside a moment?" he said to Mr. Thompson.

"I'll stay with Alex," Mrs. Thompson said as she moved to his side, "we can get acquainted."

Alex lay on the small table, exhausted. Everything was weighing down on him and he didn't know what to do. His body was tired and bruised, and he couldn't think straight past the throbbing in his head. He squeezed his eyes shut tight, but the tears trickled slowly down the side of his strained, white face. Mrs. Thompson saw the struggle on Alex's face, although he tried to turn away so she wouldn't see it. Her heart went out to the small boy who lay there, trying to be brave. She walked around the table and reached down to embrace Alex. "It's going to be all right, honey," she said. "Where's your mama?"

Alex took one look at the kind, caring woman leaning over him, and for just a moment he lost it. The tears ran freely now, and without thinking, he blurted out, "I don't know!"

Mrs. Thompson tried not to appear startled. Mr. Thompson had told her about Alex, and she knew the circumstances surrounding him were a bit strange, but could this child be lost? "What do you mean, Alex, have you run away from home, or gotten lost?"

Alex suddenly realized that he had said more than he should have. Fear began to stalk the pain, and Alex withdrew. He couldn't let Mrs. Thompson find out about where he lived or that he didn't know if his mother was alive or dead. He didn't even know his own *name* for sure. Somehow he had to get out of here and get back to the church where he could lie down. "No ma'am, I'm fine," he said quietly to Mrs. Thompson.

Outside in the hall, David spoke to his father about Alex. "What's the story here?" he asked his dad. "I can't figure it out."

Mr. Thompson replied, "He's been helping me out at the store for the last week or so, but he doesn't say much at all. He's polite and works hard, but he obviously doesn't have much of a home. He was so dirty the first day I saw him, and he was wearing torn, dirty clothing and shoes that were too small. He worked all day for a pair of shoes and was thrilled to get them. He found a pouch with coins and money in it while he was unloading merchandise for me, and he gave it back. I had to coax him to take some of the money. He was hungry and dirty and scared. He came back and washed windows for me, and was tickled when I let him take a shower to get cleaned up, and gave him a bag of old clothes that I thought would fit him. I don't know his last name, or address or anything. I have been researching the Internet and library for articles about a lost or runaway boy, but so far I haven't found anything in this area."

"Oh Dad!" David shook his head. "Another stray animal you've taken in."

"Well, David, what was I supposed to do? At first I thought he was one of the gang of boys who threw rocks at the store, but he obviously isn't. I'm telling you, there's something strange here. He gets a dazed look in his eyes sometimes, like he's daydreaming or something, but then he shakes it off. And he's one of the hardest working kids I've ever seen. What do you think happened to him?"

"Well, I'd guess that someone worked him over, or he got in a fight," David replied. "Whatever it was, he doesn't want us to know. The boy needs some rest and tender loving care. He's thin and weak right now, and he's got to be in considerable pain. There's no way he should be working or even walking around."

"What do you think about us inviting him to stay with us for a couple of days?" Mr. Thompson suggested. "You know your mom would love fussing over him. She hasn't had you around to do that for quite some time now."

"Oh, she still tries!" David laughed. "I think it would be great for both of them, if he'll do it. What do you think the chances are? Are you sure there aren't parents around somewhere? I could call child protective services."

"I just don't know. I think he might run if more strangers show up," Mr. Thompson said, shaking his head, "but we can't just leave him on the sidewalk. I could try the no-nonsense approach and tell him he's staying with us and it's doctor's orders. Maybe it will at least bring out more information from him."

"Well, I think it's worth a shot." David replied. "He certainly needs care, and he could use a haircut too. I'm sure Mom would love to get her scissors out. Let's go see what we can do."

As the doctor and Mr. Thompson returned to the examining room, Alex began to fret. The pain was making him feel sick, but he had to do something. He tried to sit up, but he fell back with a groan. "Okay," Mr. Thompson said gruffly, "that's it!" Everyone looked at him with varying degrees of concern. "Alex, are your parents or any other responsible adult able to take care of you?"

Alex blinked quickly, trying to think and clear his vision at the same time. "N-no, Sir." It was all he could manage to get out.

"Fine," Mr. Thompson responded. "Then you are coming home with us. Irene, do you have any problem looking after this youngster for a couple of days?"

Mrs. Thompson beamed. "No problem at all!" She patted Alex's knee as he looked on in dismay.

"I think that's a great idea," the doctor added. Turning to Alex, he said gently, "Son, these are my parents. They're good people. You need some care right now, some good food, and rest. Can you put up with them for a couple of days?"

Alex looked at them all, gathered around him: Mr. Thompson trying to be stern, Mrs. Thompson smiling, and their son, the concerned doctor. He thought about being part of a family atmosphere for a few days, at least until he felt a little better. No hiding, no worrying, no hunger... someone else to look after of him for a change. He hurt everywhere, even just sitting there breathing. Who was going to know or care anyway? Before he could stop, he heard himself saying, "I-I guess it would be all right if you really want to."

Mrs. Thompson didn't give Alex a chance to change his mind, and Mr. Thompson must have been thinking the exact same thing. One on either side of the table, they lifted Alex down, and each of them put an arm around him and hustled him out to Mrs. Thompson car. They tucked him into the front seat, hooked his seat belt carefully around his tattered body, and shut the door. With a wink at his son David, who had followed them out the door, Mr. Thompson hopped into the backseat and Mrs. Thompson gave David a quick hug and got behind the wheel. Before he could even think twice about anything, Alex was on his way to the Thompsons'.

13

FAMILY LIFE

Mrs. Thompson dropped Mr. Thompson off to get his truck and chatted happily as she drove along. She told Alex all about the neighborhood that they lived in where they had raised their son David. She explained that David had always wanted to be a doctor. How, as a child, he was always fixing things. "He wanted to mend everything from toys and stuffed animals to a stray kitten that he found huddled in the garage," she told Alex. "But he lives on his own now, with a beautiful wife and a baby on the way," she rambled on. "You can stay in his old room. It's still got lots of 'boy things' and is right next to the extra bathroom. It even has a television, and David's old Nintendo game. Do you like to watch television?"

Alex thought about all of the television sets he had seen in the window of the shop with the barber pole the day before. It seemed like months ago now. "I guess so," he replied.

"That's fine then," Mrs. Thompson continued without a pause, "there'll be plenty of time for that as long as you get enough rest. What do you like to eat? I could bake some chicken or fish for dinner, or spaghetti and meatballs or pork chops...what do you like, Alex? Alex?" But Alex had dozed off. The exhaustion had finally overtaken him, and the shot that the doctor had given him had relaxed him enough to induce sleep. Mrs. Thompson smiled and continued on her way.

Alex slept until they reached the Thompsons'. Mrs. Thompson pushed the button to open the garage and pulled the car in. Mr. Thompson pulled into the driveway right behind them. Alex roused himself and looked around. The garage seemed huge to him after the small confines of his little bell tower room. Mr. Thompson opened Alex's door and helped him out of the car. Mrs. Thompson bustled around them, unlocking the door to the house. Alex stepped into the spacious, comfort of the Thompsons' home. The Thompsons led him through a long, wide hallway that must serve as a laundry. Alex noticed a small bathroom at the end, spying a shower with bright yellow, fluffy towels hanging on the door. They continued on into a huge open area, where a kitchen gleamed white and shiny at the front of the house, and a large open living area sprawled toward the back. A television the size of a small movie screen covered one wall, surrounded by an overstuffed chair and sofa in warm browns and earth tones. Alex looked around in awe as they passed through the room toward another hallway that led to bedrooms.

The bedroom where Alex was to stay was charming. It was at the front of the house, with a full-length window looking out into the lawn and street. Through the side window Alex saw a lush, green forest. The bed seemed huge to Alex, made of a dark, burgundy wood with square posts on all fours corners. It was covered with a big, quilted comforter in a multitude of colors. Four large pillows in matching tones filled the space at the head of the bed, and a large, scruffy-looking teddy bear leaned against them. A large nightstand in the same wood stood next to the bed. The room was filled with "boy" things. A bookshelf from floor to ceiling held all the treasures of growing up. Books, games, a rock collection, models, trophies, and pictures sat on the shelves, just waiting to be explored. An entertainment center in the corner housed a television set, DVD/ CD player, and the Nintendo game that Mrs. Thompson had mentioned. A large, comfy chair sat in the other corner, with a small table and lamp beside it. *What a great place to grow up!* Alex thought.

As he stood in the doorway looking around, an image flickered into his thoughts. He imagined a much smaller room, with a bed and dresser. The covers were rumpled, and as he watched, "the woman" came around the side of the bed to straighten them. She smiled at Alex as she lifted a tattered, gray bear from the floor and tossed it at him. Alex reached out as if to catch the bear…into nothingness. He shook his head as the image faded and saw Mr. and Mrs. Thompson looking at him with concern.

"What is it, son?" Mr. Thompson asked with an arm around Alex's shoulder.

"N-nothing, sir," Alex stammered. Dismay was written on his pale, bruised face.

"Come on, honey," Mrs. Thompson said as she ushered Alex into the room toward the chair. "Sit down here and let's get those shoes off and get into bed. You need more rest."

Alex didn't argue. He was too tired, and too sad. She carefully untied and removed his shoes (the very ones that Mr. Thompson had given him the first day they met) as Mr. Thompson turned down the bed. She scrounged around in the closet and finally came out with an old pair of pajamas that had once been David's. She laid them at the foot of the bed. "There is a bathroom right next door where you can change, then it's into bed for you, young man."

"Why don't I help Alex here for a moment, Irene," suggested Mr. Thompson. "Maybe he would like some milk or juice or something?"

"That's a great idea, I'll be right back."

As Mrs. Thompson hurried to get him something to drink, Mr. Thompson carefully helped Alex remove the soiled jeans and shirt. He winced when Alex flinched at the pain. He held the pajama bottoms out for Alex to step into and gently slipped Alex's arms into the top and buttoned it up over his bandaged chest. He tried to ignore the scraped up knees and battered little body. And he saw marks around his ankles that looked like rope burns. Someone had done a number on this boy. Alex looked dazed. He helped him into the bathroom and waited at the door until he was done. Then he led him the short distance back to the bedroom. Mrs. Thompson was waiting for them, and without a word, Alex drank the glass of juice she held out to him, climbed gingerly into bed with Mr. Thompson's help, and let them pull the covers up around him. He was asleep almost instantly.

Mr. and Mrs. Thompson looked at each other and quietly left the room, leaving the door ajar in case Alex should wake or cry out. Not that the boy would ask, even if he needed something. What a strange, sad young man. They both wondered what the real circumstances were surrounding Alex and spoke quietly about the possibilities. Eventually, Mr. Thompson headed back to the store and Mrs. Thompson started preparations for dinner. As she opened the refrigerator, she looked up at the clock and thought she had just about enough time to make a fresh batch of cookies before she put some chicken in to bake. Smiling, she got out the ingredients. Some big, crunchy oatmeal raisin cookies were just what the doctor ordered.

Those had always been David's favorite. She was going to have to work on fattening Alex up.

❧

On his way back to the store, Mr. Thompson could not get Alex off his mind. Where had the boy come from, and what in the world had happened to him? They didn't even know the boy's last name, for heaven sakes. Well, at least he would be safe and warm for a few days. Mr. Thompson smiled. If he knew his wife, Alex would have tender, loving care and all the cookies he could eat for as long as he stayed with them. And given his wife's previous career, he'd probably get a good haircut too! In the meantime, he'd have to dig in and extend his research on the computer. Maybe he should include some of the other cities nearby and see what he could turn up about missing boys.

❧

Alex awoke a couple of hours later to the smell of fresh cookies and baking chicken. He lay in the big, comfy bed, wondering how this had all happened. Was God watching over him? Alex had doubted the existence of God after running into the gang members on Sunday. How could a loving God let something like this happen to him? Then Alex remembered the words from church about judging others. Was he judging God? He was so confused! It made his head ache all over again. Alex tried to roll over and pull the covers up, but he groaned at the pain in his ribs. Mrs. Thompson, hovering near the doorway, heard him groan. She was beside him in seconds. "Are you okay, dear?" she asked anxiously.

"Y-yes, ma'am," Alex replied politely.

"Are you ready for a bite to eat yet? I thought some cookies and milk might hold you over till dinner. How about it? Or do you just want to sleep some more?" Mrs. Thompson rambled on nervously, twisting at her apron in a way that somehow seemed familiar to Alex.

His stomach had begun rumbling so loud that he was sure Mrs. Thompson would be able to hear it. He hadn't eaten anything this morning, and cookies and milk sounded wonderful, even amidst all the pain he was experiencing. He looked at Mrs. Thompson's anxious face and gave a tentative smile. "Cookies and milk would be really nice," he said without his usual stammer.

Mrs. Thompson beamed at him and helped him prop himself up with his pillows. She went over to the entertainment center and located the remote control and handed it to Alex. "I'll be right back," she said. "Why don't you find something you like on the television."

Alex stared blankly at the screen as she bustled from the room. *Television?* he thought to himself. *What do I like?* He turned on the power switch and started flipping through the channels. He stopped at the channel for CNN, and before he could comprehend the sports scores and basketball players flashing before him, Mrs. Thompson returned.

"Here you go, Alex," she said, placing a tray across Alex's lap. The tray contained a plate of oatmeal raisin cookies, a glass of ice cold milk, and a large, yellow banana. "This should hold you until dinner. Is there anything else you need?"

Alex looked down at the feast before him. "N-no, this is f-fine," was all he could manage. He was back to stammering again.

"Well, I won't be far, dear, you just call if you need something." She hurried back to the kitchen to check on dinner.

Alex picked up a cookie and took a bite. He had tasted Mrs. Thompson's cookies before, but these were right out of the oven and tasted heavenly. Alex washed it down with some cold milk and proceeded to finish it off. He carefully peeled the banana and continued flipping through the channels until he discovered an old *Flipper* rerun. For some reason the dolphin appealed to him, and he laid down the remote to watch. He had finished off the banana, another cookie, and the glass of milk by the end of the program. Mrs. Thompson stood watching him in the doorway. Alex looked over as the commercials started and she came in to remove the tray. He lay back on the pillows watching a silly commercial about Fruity Pebbles. Idly he looked around the room, wondering again how he came to be here. Mrs. Thompson was back in a few moments. "I thought you might want to get cleaned up, so I filled the bathtub," she said, "but if you're too sore, I can just empty it and wait until later. I thought the warm water might make you feel a little better. What do you think?"

The thought of a warm bath was more than Alex could resist. After the cookies and milk and fruit, he felt much stronger. "I'd like that," he said, struggling to push back the covers.

Mrs. Thompson pulled the covers back and helped Alex out of bed. He wobbled just a bit as he stood up. "I put out fresh towels and soap," Mrs. Thompson said as she unbuttoned his pajama top, slipped it off, and laid it on the bed. "Can you get in by yourself?"

"Y-yes," Alex stammered again, nervously.

"Well go on then," Mrs. Thompson said, realizing that she was still a stranger to the boy, "just call me if you need help. Don't worry about the bandages. Once you are finished, put your pajama bottoms on and come on out. I'll find you some clean socks. Mr. Thompson will be home soon, and David will be coming by with some fresh bandages to check on you. He and his wife, Heather, will be joining us for dinner."

Alex walked slowly into the bathroom. Mrs. Thompson had thought of everything. A big, soft, blue towel was laid on a bench near the bathtub. Bubbles danced in the water, begging Alex to jump right in. A matching washcloth with a fresh bar of soap was waiting on the corner of the bathtub, and clean boxers were folded carefully over the edge of the sink. Alex closed the door, leaving it open just a crack so he could hear Mrs. Thompson setting the table. Gingerly, he stepped out of the pajama bottoms and boxers he had on. Carefully, he stepped over the tub, wincing at the pain it cost him to climb in. He lowered his aching body into the warm, sudsy water. Whew! Once the effort of getting in was over, he sighed in relief. The warm water soaked through the bandages and warmed him all over. He slid down to wet his hair and let the water rinse off his face. The bubbles smarted as they rinsed over the welts on his face and clung to the stitches in his chin, although he was careful not to get them too wet. Alex gritted his teeth, and picked up the soap and washcloth. He wet the cloth, soaped it up, and gently washed his battered face. The warm water and soap actually felt good, and it was a relief to get rid of the salty grit from perspiration and dust on the walk over to the store. The stinging on his scraped knees dulled and the warmth of the water soothed his aching body. He wanted to stay there forever! Eventually, Alex felt the water turning cool and knew he was going to have to endure the climb out of the tub. He opened the drain and managed slowly and painfully to stand up and reach over to the towel. He dried off as best he could and made it out of the tub. He stepped into the slightly baggy boxers and pulled the pajama bottoms over his damp body. The effort cost him all of the stamina he could muster, and since Mrs. Thompson was still busy with dinner, he headed back to the bedroom. He wrapped the towel around his wet bandages and managed to climb up onto the bed. He closed his eyes and drifted back to sleep.

Alex was dreaming that the woman was sitting on the side of his bed rubbing lotion on his back and chest, when his eyes flew open in startled pain! Instead of the woman, he found himself looking into the kindly eyes of the doctor.

"Hey, Alex, I'm sorry about that!" David said softly. "I didn't mean to hurt you."

Alex stared blankly at David as he finished removing the wet bandages and replaced them with dry ones. Mr. Thompson stood in the doorway looking on, with a petite, brunette by his side. Alex closed his eyes, unwilling to let go of the dream and face reality.

"How are you feeling, Alex?" David asked him. "Does your head hurt?"

Alex barely managed a nod. All he wanted was to be left alone to remember his dream.

David picked up a pill and glass of water from the nightstand and handed them to Alex. "Take this, son," he said, "it will help with the pain."

Alex managed to take the pill and hand the water back to the doctor. He wanted nothing more than to get back under the covers.

David could almost read his thoughts. Turning to his wife and Mr. Thompson, he said, "Alex should probably stay in bed for tonight and rest. Let's have Mom bring his dinner in here." To Alex he said, "We'll give you a few minutes to let that medicine work. Are you okay with eating in your room tonight?" Again Alex nodded. David helped him stand up and removed the damp towel from the bed. He almost lifted Alex back into the bed and pulled the covers around him. "I'll see you a little later," he said softly, and left the room followed by his wife and father.

Alex closed his eyes tightly as they left, trying to remember. The pain in his head was making it too difficult. He felt like the lady he kept seeing had to be his mother. So where was she? He knew from some of the memories that she cared about him. She had baked him cookies and shopped with him and made his bed. But then he remembered her telling him she was sorry and packing boxes. A feeling of rejection washed over him, and his eyes filled with tears. Had she left him? Why had he been in the dump, with his head all banged up? Alex gritted his teeth against the pain and memories. There was no way he could connect the woman he kept remembering with someone who would hurt him physically. He closed his eyes and waited for the pain to ease.

A knock on the bedroom door caused him to open his eyes. David's wife Heather was standing at the door with the tray that Mrs. Thompson had used earlier. She smiled brightly as she came into the room. The smell of home-cooked food filled the air and made Alex's mouth water in spite of his condition. It seemed like he was always hungry. Heather placed the tray on the nightstand and came over to help Alex scoot up against the pillows. She tucked the covers gently around him as she introduced herself. Alex noticed her rounded belly and knew that she was going to have a baby soon, as Mrs. Thompson had mentioned earlier. Heather placed the tray across Alex's lap and asked if there was anything else he needed. "No thank you," he replied quietly.

Heather smiled at Alex, and he was instantly warmed by her presence. "I'll be back in a few moments to check on you then, okay?" Heather asked.

Alex just nodded his head. As Heather left, Alex looked at the food on his tray in amazement! Baked chicken, mashed potatoes, and fresh, steamed green beans were arranged beautifully on a shiny, white plate. A smaller matching plate held a fresh, warm roll with butter and jam. Strawberries with whip cream added a splash of color to the meal. A tall, cold glass of chocolate milk enticed him to begin. Alex felt like he had died and gone to heaven, but as he reached for his fork, the pain in his side brought him quickly back to reality. Still, in the time that Alex had been on his own, he had not seen anything even close to the meal sitting before him. Other than the couple of times he had eaten at the Corner Café, nothing could compare to this.

The evening passed quickly after dinner. Alex managed to get down almost every crumb of his dinner. Heather and David came back and visited with Alex while Mr. and Mrs. cleaned up the dishes. They chatted easily with Alex, and David showed him how to work the controls for the Nintendo game. Afterward, David picked Alex up and carried him out to the sofa so they could all visit. Alex was very quiet. He watched and listened as they all laughed and talked, but rarely joined in. Heather did manage to coax a smile from him a couple of times, and Alex felt more and more comfortable sitting next to her on the sofa. After about an hour, it was obvious that Alex was getting worn out and David and Heather were ready to leave for home. David carried Alex back to bed and gave him another dose of medicine to help with the pain. Alex was exhausted, but for the first time in a long while, he felt safe and protected. Mr. and Mrs. Thompson came in to say good night, and as they all stood around the bed, Alex suddenly knew without a doubt that God was indeed watching over him. Somehow, even in these dire circumstances, He had blessed him with a loving family to care for him. It just couldn't be an accident. Still, as the medicine took effect, and his eyes grew heavy, his last thoughts were filled with the woman of his dreams.

And miles and miles away, that very woman lay sobbing for the little boy she could not find, missing him with every breath that was in her.

14

HEALING AND A HAIRCUT!

The next few days passed quickly for Alex. He slept a lot, and the cuts and scrapes and bruises all began to heal. His ribs were still very tender, and the stitches on his chin were beginning to itch. Dr. David was coming over on Friday to remove them, and Alex was beginning to get antsy about what was happening back at the bell tower. He was even a little worried about his belongings, especially the money he had left. He still needed it to survive. Living here at the Thompsons' was like being in another world, and he knew eventually he would have to go back to the reality of the way things were. Mrs. Thompson, or "Tilly" as Mr. Thompson called her affectionately (especially when she got flustered), had hinted several times about wanting to know more about him, and Alex was having a hard time putting her off. She was such a warm and caring lady, and

Alex already felt close to her. Alex saw Mr. Thompson looking at him thoughtfully at times too, and he knew he must have so many questions. Once, long into the night, when Alex got up to use the bathroom, he saw him sitting at the computer intently reading the screen. Was he finding the answers to his questions?

Alex had questions too. His memory was increasing in bits and pieces, but nothing made any real sense. He still felt uncomfortable with "Alex" and still had no idea what his last name was. How could he tell them that? He knew now that the lady in his dreams had to be his mother. The night before he had been dreaming of her taking him to a movie, and when they were suddenly surrounded by the crowd at the end of the movie, he lost sight of her. He had sat up in bed reaching out and crying "Mom!" Mr. Thompson had come running from the bedroom on the other side of the bathroom to see what was wrong. After he saw that Alex was okay and only dreaming, he went back to bed. Alex had lain awake for a long time trying to remember. He had finally fallen back to sleep, but he was convinced that the lady was his mother. Was she looking for him? If he could only remember more, he might be able to find her.

Alex was able to get up and around a little bit now, and was exploring the shelves in the bedroom. He picked up an old volume of *Tom Sawyer* and leafed through a few pages. As he read the first lines of one of the chapters, he realized that it was familiar. Excited, he sat down in the chair and began to read. Mrs. Thompson looked in on him later, only to discover him sitting there reading with a look of amazement on his face!

"What is it, Alex?" she asked.

"I know this story!" Alex exclaimed. "I'm sure I've read it before."

Mrs. Thompson looked confused. "Is that a surprise to you?" she asked Alex.

Alex looked up blankly at her. He realized that she didn't know about his loss of memory, and suddenly he felt guilty.

Mrs. Thompson recognized that look, and sitting next to him on the big chair, she took his hand. "Honey, what is it?"

The look on her face was almost Alex's undoing. How could he tell her? He found himself wanting to. "It's just that..." His head started pounding and he couldn't think straight. He wanted to tell her everything. He started again. "It's just...nothing...nothing." Mrs. Thompson knew there was more. They both knew. But along with being kind and loving, Mrs. Thompson was patient. Alex would tell her in his own time.

On Thursday, Mrs. Thompson decided to approach Alex about his hair. She had been itching to get her scissors out and see what she could do to clean up his shaggy locks. She noticed him pulling at it sometimes and pushing it out of his eyes. "I used to cut hair at the hospital, and I still do occasionally for some of David's patients," she told Alex at lunch. "I was wondering if you would like your hair cut.

I thought you might want to get spiffed up a bit before David comes over tomorrow to take out your stitches. I think Heather is coming again too. What do you say? I do a pretty good job, if I say so myself, and your hair is getting a little shaggy. Want to give it a try?"

Alex just sat there. He wanted to tell her that he had been looking for a barber the night he got beaten up, but he couldn't. He reached up and felt the shaggy hair hanging on his neck and smiled.

"Come on, son," Mrs. Thompson said easily, "let's see what we can do." Mrs. Thompson guided Alex toward the end of the house on the other side of the kitchen. She opened a set of French doors and they passed through a small sitting room. Her "shop" consisted of a small room, with a sink and mirror above a salon-type chair. A small set of bins on wheels contained all the paraphernalia required for cutting hair. Brushes, combs, scissors and even a small razor were nestled in one bin, neatly folded towels in another, while shampoos, conditioners, hairspray, and other miscellaneous bottles and jars covered the top. Mrs. Thompson helped Alex up into the chair and fastened a large wrap around his neck. "You tell me if anything hurts, okay?" she asked Alex. She pumped up the chair so he was at the right level, and tipped the chair back over the sink. Turning on the water, she adjusted the temperature and picked up the sprayer to wet his hair. Very gently she smoothed on shampoo, as she supported his neck with her other hand. Letting go of the sprayer, she used both hands to massage the shampoo into Alex scalp. *Was that matted blood in his hair?* As she gently washed his hair, she could feel the bumps and scrapes on the back of his head. In one spot, there was an older, ridged area that she could feel with her fingertips. The roughness of the scalp around it told her that it had not healed cleanly and was not very old. *What had this boy been through?* "Are you doing okay, Alex?" she asked a bit anxiously. Alex just nodded his head. His ribs still hurt with every move, but he was not going to complain. He wanted a haircut! Mrs. Thompson expertly rinsed his hair and gently toweled it dry. She could actually see a scraped area on the back of his head now, where it had scabbed over. Careful of that area, she combed out Alex's hair and picked up her scissors.

Alex sat stiffly in the chair. Though his scalp was still tender in the back, it felt so good to have his hair washed properly that he was determined not to cringe. As he sat there, he wondered if Mrs. Thompson would notice the recently healed area at the base of his skull. He knew it must show, because at times it still ached dully. And he had felt stickiness in his hair after the boys had dragged him into the old house. He knew there might be scabs or something, would she notice? But, Mrs. Thompson snipped away at his hair without commenting. Alex finally relaxed a bit, relieved to have his hair cut into a more manageable style. All that trouble looking for a barbershop, and here he sat at the Thompsons' getting a haircut. If he had only asked Mr.

Thompson about a barber that day at his shop… If he had paid more attention to where he was going… If he hadn't gotten away from those boys…Alex shivered.

"Are you okay, Alex? Alex?" Mrs. Thompson voice was concerned.

Suddenly, Alex realized that she was speaking to him. "I-I'm f-fine," he stammered. He looked at Mrs. Thompson's questioning eyes. When he didn't say anything, she turned the chair so he could see his hair.

"Well, what do you think?"

Alex looked in the mirror in disbelief. His hair looked neat and trim and *clean*! But his face was a mess! Alex saw two long scratches on one cheek and stitches in his chin, with black, blue, and yellow coloring surrounding them. Tears filled his eyes as he remembered.

Without a word, Mrs. Thompson removed the wrap and helped Alex down from the chair. She led him back to the small sofa in the sitting room and put her arms around him. "Oh, Alex," she said and she comforted him, "what happened to you?"

15

SO CLOSE TO CONFESSION

Alex looked up at the women who had been caring for him for the last few days. He saw nothing but kindness, understanding, and caring in her warm, brown eyes. He had been alone for so long, with no one to share his troubles with. Could he trust this woman? The overwhelming desire for help and the encouraging look on Mrs. Thompson face was his answer. Still, he hesitated. What would happen if they knew the truth? What would they think of him? He just couldn't confess it all yet. Once again, he kept it to himself, mumbling something about needing to use the bathroom.

Mrs. Thompson saw his struggle and understood. Without another word, she gave Alex a warm hug and told him to go on then. She began cleaning up the area as he made his way to the bathroom. Alex looked at himself in the mirror again. Was that what he looked like? The haircut looked amazing, in spite of his battered face. He felt his neck in wonder, so happy that the long, scraggly hair was gone! Would he ever remember everything and be a normal kid again? Would he ever find his mom? As his thoughts started pounding into his head again, he shoved them away. He wanted to enjoy this brief moment of happiness and feeling of content. He had loving people around him, plenty to eat and much to be thankful for. He decided to read some more from the *Tom Sawyer* book he had discovered and enjoy the day for a change. He was glad Dr. David would be taking the stitches out tomorrow and was happily anticipating seeing him and Heather again.

The next day, Alex enjoyed reading for a couple of hours and even thought about going outside. Memories of what had happened over the past few weeks countered that thought and kept him inside the safety of the house. Mrs. Thompson made him a tasty egg salad sandwich for lunch along with another one of her wonderful cookies, and encouraged him to look through a drawer full of movies and pick one out that he might like to see. She settled him on the couch, ever careful of his sore ribs, with something to drink nearby in case he got thirsty and left him to watch the movie he had selected. It was one about a dog who played basketball, and it seemed like only yesterday that David had watched it himself. Where did the time go? She headed back to the kitchen to work on the evening meal, glancing over the counter every now and then where she could see Alex relaxed and smiling for a change. At one point she actually heard him laugh a little at one of the antics of the dog in the movie. She felt tears welling up in her eyes as she thought about what this little boy had been forced to endure.

Mr. Thompson came home early that night. After washing up and changing clothes, he came over and sat near Alex to watch the rest of the movie. He marveled at Alex's haircut and ruffled his new hair a bit before he settled down to watch. He realized he had actually missed the boy at the store and was happy to have him here when he got home. Still he worried about what was to come of Alex. He knew they couldn't keep him here once he was completely healed and wondered when and if Alex would share more with them. He had to get back on the computer tonight and keep up the research. He hadn't found anything so far in Illinois, so he was going to start looking at the news in Michigan cities nearby, hoping something would give him a clue. He dosed in his chair, not noticing the smile that Alex turned his way when he began to snore softly.

Shortly after the movie ended, Alex returned it to the drawer and wondered over to the kitchen to see if there was anything he could do. He scooted up onto a bar stool at the counter, watching Mrs. Thompson prepare the meatballs for their spaghetti dinner. "Would you like to cut up some vegetables for salad?" she asked Alex. He nodded yes and wondered if he would know how. She placed a cutting board on the counter, along with a couple of tomatoes and cucumbers and a bowl to place them in. Alex picked up the knife she handed him and the first cucumber. Carefully he peeled off the outer skin and set it aside, slicing the rest of cucumber in even slices. He was in another place, with his mom laughing beside him, showing him how to do it! He smiled and looked up startled, hoping that Mrs. Thompson hadn't seen him. She went about her work at the stove, and he breathed a little easier as he finished cutting up the veggies and placing them in the bowl. Mrs. Thompson marveled at how well he did, and had noticed his dreamy look and the smile. She just knew this boy had a mother somewhere…someone who had shown him how to do all the things he found himself doing…someone who loved him and missed him. They had to find a way to help Alex and get him to tell them what had happened!

That night Dr. David came over and removed the stitches from Alex's chin. "Good as new!" he proclaimed, as he pulled out the last stitch. Alex ran into the bathroom to look in the mirror. His face was looking so much better! The bruising was turning yellow and fading away and he was starting to look like a healthy, happy little boy. He walked back into the living room repeating his thanks and settling down next to Heather. She smelled so good, and something about her stirred memories that he longed for.

After dinner they played a game of cards, and Alex actually joined in and was able to learn quickly how to play. Dr. David and Mr. Thompson discussed something about their church as they played, and Alex listened intently. They were discussing why God let bad things happen to good people, as someone they knew had been hurt badly in a car accident. Mr. Thompson insisted that God didn't make bad things happen, people did. Because of freedom of choice, people made choices that resulted in difficult situations, even harm to themselves. In those times, people needed to turn to God for comfort and healing, not blame him for what had happened. Dr. David agreed for the most part, and Alex heard him ask his father to pray for the family. Once again Alex felt like God was real and watching over him.

All too soon Dr. David and Heather were getting ready to leave. As they hugged Mr. and Mrs. Thompson good-bye, they included Alex and both gave him a hug. Heather kissed Alex on the top of his head after she hugged him and said good-bye. Alex was overwhelmed and tired. He told the Thompsons he was ready for bed and said good night. He still tired easily, so no questions were asked. He slipped into the bedroom and quietly changed into his pajamas. His chin was throbbing a bit from getting the stitches out. After a few minutes, Mrs. Thompson came in with a glass of water and a pain pill that Dr. David had left for him. "Why don't you take this, honey," she said, "it will help you if your chin hurts and you should sleep better." Alex took the pill and mumbled another good night as Mrs. Thompson left the room. Within a short time, he was fast asleep. His dreams were vague and confusing at first; he dreamed he was playing cards with his mom, or was it Heather? Letting it go, he sank into a heavy, dreamless sleep for the rest of the night.

16

THE TRUTH IS OUT!

Alex got stronger and stronger over the next couple of days. The regular meals and safety of his surroundings helped immensely. He was sorting through a box of marbles that he found on the shelf in the bedroom one day, feeling a bit lonely and aching for his memories to ALL come back. As he sifted through the marbles, he remembered something… "Mr. Alan," someone said sternly, "please put the marbles away. Lunch is over and it's time to get back to class."

What? Alex wondered. *Mr. Alan?* Did she mean Alex? Could his name be Alex Alan? In the anxiety of the moment, the box of marbles fell from his hands and scattered across the shelf.

Hearing the noise, Mrs. Thompson poked her head in the door to see if everything was okay. Seeing Alex's face, she knew immediately it wasn't. "What is it, Alex?" she asked.

Alex was so confused and the memory loss was weighing on him. What was he supposed to do?

Alex looked at Mrs. Thompson and saw the concern on her face. He knew she cared about him. He knew she only wanted to help. He opened his mouth to explain his memory of the marbles, and before he even realized fully what was happening, the whole story came pouring out. The dump where he woke up…the struggles to find food and clothes and shoes…living in the bell tower…finding Mr. Thompson's store and working so hard to get new shoes…finding the money and the gang chasing him…the Corner Café and Carol…going to church…and finally the boys beating him up and dragging him to the house. He told her about the little, crippled man helping him. Once he got started, Alex couldn't stop. He went on and on and on, needing to get it all out. Everything had been crammed into his head for weeks and weeks. Mrs. Thompson sat listening in shock. Tears ran down her face, but she brushed them away and gently encouraged Alex. Expressions flitted across her face at different times, but Alex hardly noticed. He needed to talk. He needed to cry. He needed someone to care. He needed his mom. He told Mrs. Thompson about his dreams of "the lady."

"I just know it has to be my mom," he finished anxiously. "Do you think she might be looking for me, or be hurt or be lost like me?"

Mrs. Thompson sat back and looked at the young boy sitting there. What was he, ten or eleven? Obviously, he didn't even know that. What a brave child. Tears came to her eyes again. She couldn't help but think about the horrible things this child had experienced in the last month or so, all by himself. And here he sat in baggy, borrowed clothing (Mr. Thompson had brought home a few things from the store), with his bruised face and anxious words. And after everything, his first thought was about his mother. Mrs. Thompson took his hands in hers. "Alex," she said quietly, "we have to get help."

"What do you mean?" Alex replied.

"We need to look into all that you've told me. Can you find the dump where you woke up the first day?"

Alex nodded affirmatively.

"Good. We need to tell Mr. Thompson, and call the police and check the newspapers to see if there is anyone missing. If your mother is out there somewhere, she has to be looking for you." Alex looked up at Mrs. Thompson with hope. She let go of his hands and picked up the phone from a table beside the sofa and dialed Mr. Thompson at the store. After a brief explanation, with Alex watching anxiously, she hung up the phone. "Are you okay?" she asked Alex. He nodded. She took his hands again. "Listen, honey, it's going to be all right. You've become part of this family and we aren't going to let you face this all alone now, okay?"

Alex looked at her in disbelief! "But all my stuff is at the church, and you don't even know me!" he cried in dismay, tears forming again in his eyes in spite of himself. "I d-didn't mean to cause trouble for you," he mumbled.

"Now listen, Alex," Mrs. Thompson said firmly. "You are not causing us trouble. We care about you, son. We *like* you! Do you want to go to the church and get your things?" Alex still looked doubtful. "Are you okay with staying here, Alex?" Mrs. Thompson asked. "I know we haven't known each other long, but I just can't bear thinking about you living alone. I certainly don't want anyone else coming across you and calling authorities or harming you."

Alex made up his mind. "I w-want to stay with you if it's okay," he managed with only the slightest stutter. "I mean if it's really okay, and not too much trouble."

Standing up quickly before he could change his mind, Mrs. Thompson grabbed his hand and said, "Then let's go get your belongings right now!"

17

BACK AT THE CHURCH

Alex was very quiet on the way to the church. He was thinking about everything that had happened to him and remembering how safe he had felt when he discovered the bell tower and realized he had a place to go. He was thinking about God and the Thompsons and the gang of boys who were determined to terrorize him. He was beginning to realize that nothing happened by chance. If they hadn't chased him he wouldn't have discovered the church. He wouldn't have met Dr. Dave and Heather and lived with the Thompsons. He thought about the little wizened man and how he hadn't felt his touch when he was untying him. Was it possible that there really were angels and God had been looking after him the whole time? Alex looked out the window in anticipation of visiting the one place that had given him sanctuary.

When they reached the church, Alex finally spoke. "Would you come with me?" he asked Mrs. Thompson.

"Of course I will!" She parked the car in the lot behind the church and they headed in.

Alex didn't notice her look of surprise, and she didn't enlighten him. There was no one in the sanctuary when they entered. Alex knew it would be pretty well deserted at this time of day. "It's this way," he whispered to Mrs. Thompson, leading to the back of the church. He pushed aside the draperies and started up the first set of stairs. When he got to the balcony, he led Mrs. Thompson to the second door and started up the stairs to the bell tower. Slowly, panting by now, they made their way to the top. Alex opened the door to the bell tower and stepped inside. In disbelief, he looked around.

Someone had been there! Everything was neat as a pin, but Alex could tell it was different. And there was a strong smell of disinfectant in the room. Someone had been cleaning! Alex rushed over to the door on the back wall and opened it up. His face lit up! No one had been in here. It was just as he had left it on that fateful day. He reached down to pick up the dirty, bloody shirt that he had left where it fell the morning he had gone to Mr. Thomson's store, and he started to tremble.

Mrs. Thompson was watching from across the room, but when she saw Alex's distress, she rushed over and took the shirt. Stuffing it quickly under her arm, she pulled a couple of large bags out of her purse and shook them out. "Let's get all of your stuff packed up." She said quietly, "Are you ready?"

Alex nodded, and they went quickly to work. Alex pulled out his boxes of clothing, along with the bag of stuff that Carol had given him. He picked up the extra shoes and books. He lifted the wooden crate and found his money pouch and food just as he had left them. He stuffed the money pouch in his pocket and piled the food into the smaller bag that Mrs. Thompson handed him, to be thrown away. The food had spoiled, but thankfully he was no longer in need of every crumb. Mrs. Thompson didn't say a word as she helped Alex gather his things and pack them into the large plastic bags. While she knew some of the stuff was not worth keeping, she also realized that these things were all that Alex had and that they had been painstakingly gathered and hoarded. They could sort through it all when they got back to the house. Her heart went out to the little boy, standing there in his worn, used clothing with his fresh washed haircut looking as out of place as he did. How had this child survived this long?

Once everything was packed up, Alex picked up the blankets that he had used and tried to shake them out. He knew that they were soiled from his use. He looked with concern at Mrs. Thompson. "S-Should I put these back?"

Mrs. Thompson took the small blankets from Alex. "Why don't we take them home and I'll wash them up and bring them back."

Alex nodded soberly and handed them to Mrs. Thompson. "Thank you" was all he could manage to say. He quietly moved the cots back the way they had been when he found them and returned the crate to the back of the storage area. He filled it back up with the small toys and books that he had emptied out of the crate so long ago. Looking around, he nodded and backed out of the area. With one last sad look, he closed the door. Looking around the room, he searched for understanding. He walked over to the cables that supported the large bell. He wished that the bell was down in the room where he could touch it once more.

Sensing his distress, Mrs. Thompson walked over and put an arm around his shoulders. "We can come back any time you like, Alex," she said. "Let's get this stuff downstairs and out in the car." Each of them picked up one of the large white bags and left the bell tower with all of his belongings.

Mrs. Thompson and Alex looked awkward hauling the large, white bags down the stairs and out to the car, especially since they had to go so slow for Alex. Luckily, no one saw them. Mrs. Thompson had already decided on what she would say if someone approached them, but they made it out of the church without seeing a soul. Unknown to either of them, the elderly priest at the front corner of the church watched knowingly as they left.

18

THE POLICE

When Mrs. Thompson and Alex returned to the house, Mr. Thompson met them at the door. He seemed a bit upset, but very happy to see them. He gave Alex a hug, looking over his shoulder at Mrs. Thompson with a question in his eyes. "Well, Alex, I'm glad you finally opened up about being lost. I knew you would tell us your story when the time was right. Are you okay, son?" Alex nodded, looking down and trying not to cry. It was obvious that the whole ordeal had worn him out. Mrs. Thompson suggested that Alex take a break and play Nintendo, read, or simply rest in his room for a little bit. Alex gladly escaped to his room, feeling very sad about leaving the church, although not really understanding why. He sprawled out on the bed trying to recapture the safety he had felt at the church. He thought about finding the church when the gang was chasing him and having a place to sleep safely and to store his few belongings. He thought about the times he simply lay there and dreamt of the lady…those dreams that made him long for and believe that he had a better life that included a mother who loved him. All of those memories were mixed up with and part of the church. He hated to leave it all behind forever. Struggling with all of the emotions involved in telling Mrs. Thompson about what had happened, and getting his belongings and leaving the church, had simply worn him out! He closed his eyes and fell asleep.

Voices woke Alex, and for a panic-stricken moment, he was afraid that he was back in the dream. The voices were getting loud and Alex recognized both Mr. and Mrs. Thompson's voices, along with a couple of strangers' voices. "Why in the world would you want to take this boy into custody and put him through any more than he has already been through!" he heard Mrs. Thompson exclaim. "That just seems utterly ridiculous!"

"There must be something you can do," Mr. Thompson stated calmly. "The boy is welcome to stay with us until you find his mother."

Alex jumped up quietly and peered through the door of his room trying to see who they were talking to. He could just make out the backs of two policemen who were talking to the Thompsons. "I'm sorry, sir, but the boy will have to come with us. You have no right to hold him here."

Now Mr. Thompson began to turn red in the face and pointed his finger at the policeman. "Look here, young man…"

Alex didn't wait to hear any more. There was no way he was going anywhere with some strange policemen! He had managed to avoid policemen for a couple of months now and there was no way one was getting his hands on him if he could help it!

Alex quickly grabbed an old backpack out of the closet in his room that Mrs. Thompson had given him to keep a few things in and grabbing whatever he could think of started stuffing things into it. Extra clothes, toothbrush and paste, comb, and extra shoes were all jumbled inside. He looked around frantically at what had become "his room," struggling with leaving it all. Why was this happening? First he had given up the sanctuary of the church, now he was being forced to leave the Thompsons' house. The sense of loss was so overwhelming it brought tears to his eyes. For a fleeting second he wondered, "God, what have I done to deserve this?" The second passed, and with one last, frantic look, he snatched up the small blanket that lay at the end of his bed and grabbed socks and underwear from a stack of clean laundry that Mrs. Thompson had brought in and placed on his chair just that morning. He went over to the window, ignoring the conversation that seemed to be getting louder by the minute and tried pushing it open. It slid up easily and quietly as Alex glanced over his shoulder, worried that at any moment a police officer would come crashing into his room. Without hesitation, he tossed the backpack out the window and quickly climbed up on the chair to follow it. Luckily, the ground was not that far below and Alex landed with thud next to his bag. His gasped as he saw tiny stars and felt sharp pain in his side. Still, he was desperate. He grabbed his bag and was, once again, on the run!

Alex hurried to the garage, around the back of it and into the quiet neighborhood. He tried not to run, as he knew instinctively that this would only draw attention to him. Instead he walked casually heading in the direction that he knew would lead him away from the Thompsons and the police. He tried to pay attention to his surroundings, hoping to find some kind of familiar territory. He knew the basic direction of the church, since they had just driven there, but also knew that he couldn't go there yet, if ever. Tears blinded him and he almost stumbled over an uneven joint in the sidewalk. Hearing the sudden roar of a crowd, he quickly made his way across an open area to a crowd of people watching a soccer match. He stayed in the edges of the crowd, watching constantly for any signs of policemen, until it looked like the game was over. Gradually he continued to the other side of the field and slipped into a small group of buildings behind a school.

Skirting around the buildings, he started down the sidewalk making his way toward what he hoped was the direction that would eventually be familiar. It seemed like hours since he had left the Thompsons, but he knew he had to keep going until he could find a place to hide where no one could get to him. He checked out a couple of empty-looking buildings, but they were locked. He kept going. He needed to find something before dark that would provide some kind of protection, so he just kept trudging along. Suddenly remembering the pouch of money that he had stuffed in his pocket at the church, he stopped at the next convenience store he passed to get a cold drink. Taking a sip from the water he had purchased, he rounded the corner and almost smacked right into a cop! Luckily for him, the policeman was chasing someone else and didn't even notice him. He kept on past another stoplight and saw a McDonald's. Having no appetite at the moment and knowing that his money had to be rationed, he ignored the smells that made his stomach growl and kept on going, thankful for the breakfast of pancakes, eggs, and bacon that Mrs. Thompson had fixed him this morning. When he saw the old barbershop sign, he suddenly knew exactly where he was! He was headed back to the area where the boys had beaten him up and thrown him in the old house. Panicking, he started to turn around and head in the other direction, when he remembered the area in the basement of the house where he had fallen onto the mattress. He thought for a moment about the crippled man who had helped him and about all of the nooks and crannies in the house where he could hide. It was starting to get dark and he was worried about being out in this area after dark. He certainly couldn't just stand there waiting for someone to spot him.

Quickly he made his way to the spot where he could see the house. Everything was quiet, so he crept around to the back and down the steep incline that led to the lower level. Alex moved as silently as possible, fearing that at any moment those boys would come running out of nowhere and find him. At the back of the house he quickly found the spot between the two walls that led into the house. Peering into the darkness, he tried to make out the shapes inside, to ensure that nobody was lurking in the shadows. He wound his way through the maze that had led him to safety that fateful day, and finally came upon the mattress. Looking up he saw the hole in the floor above that he had fallen through. Quietly he made his way deeper into the house, fearful of every creak and crackle. He found a small room that was stacked with all types of broken down furniture, including an old sofa that he could just make out in one corner. By crawling over a pile of broken kitchen chairs, a table leaning on two legs, and skirting around a huge cupboard of some type, he could just squeeze into the corner and climb onto the sofa. The cupboard provided a sort of protection, from the rest of the room, and anyone passing by the doorway would not be able to see him back in the corner. This was going to have to do for the time being until he could get out and find something better. Everything was covered in dust and dirt, but Alex was so distraught and in so much pain that he didn't notice. He unzipped his backpack and pulled out the small blanket.

He wrapped it around his head and upper body and buried his face in the familiar smell. Tears poured down his face as he tried to resolve himself to staying in the one place that had almost been his undoing.

Back at the Thompsons' the police were winning the argument about taking Alex into police custody. They explained again and again that the law regulated these types of incidents, especially when children were involved. They would have to turn Alex over to Child Protective Services until his mother could be located, and there was no way around it. The officers promised the Thompsons they could check with them regularly to ensure he was okay, or perhaps even apply for a foster care license down the road if his mother could not be located. But they had to take him with them today. With heavy hearts, the Thompsons headed toward the bedroom to explain what was happening to Alex. When they pushed open the bedroom door and saw the open window, they knew it was too late. Once again, Alex was on the run.

19

MORE DREAMS

It was almost morning. Alex could tell because the black of night was turning to the misty gray of dawn. His head hurt, and his heart pounded to the beat, helping his blood pound out the pain. He tried to move, but his legs were numb, and as he reached down to see why, something fuzzy scurried across his arm. The rats were back! Alex awoke with a start from the memories of the dump where he had found himself that fateful day, to the same misty grayness of his dream. This time, instead of finding the rats of the dump, he saw that the fuzzy creature who had brushed his arm was a tiny kitten. As he struggled to pull his legs out from under him and sit up, three more of the little varmints scattered in every direction. Sensing the commotion, the mother cat came out from under the sofa to see what was going on. As soon as the kittens saw her, they jumped on her in an effort to get her to lie down so they could get milk! Alex watched it all with a slight smile on his face until he realized where he was. Suddenly, he sat up with a start! He had to get out of here and figure out what to do.

As he started to get up and begin the climb over broken furniture to the door, he felt a slight motion to his left. Turning slightly, he could just make out a small form beyond the sofa. Was it the mysterious little man again? Straining, he could just make him out and see that he was gesturing for him to be quiet by holding a finger to his lips and motioning for him to lie down. Something about the wizened face reminded Alex of the old pastor at the church. As Alex ducked back down on the sofa out of sight of the doorway, he heard the loud, rough voices of the gang members. They were arguing about something, as usual, but Alex couldn't make out what they were saying. From the sound of their voices, Alex guessed that they were still outside the house. After a few minutes the voices died away and Alex suspected the gang had moved on. He sat back up and looked for the man again, but he was nowhere in sight. Alex wondered briefly why this crippled little man always seemed to be there when he needed him, but his growling stomach soon told him there were other more pressing matters at hand.

Shouldering his backpack, Alex began the careful climb out of the room. When he made it to the place where he would leave the relative safety of the house, he peered out cautiously looking for the gang. Everything appeared quiet and deserted, so he made his way out of the house and up the incline to street level. Knowing that the McDonald's was not far away, he headed in that direction, staying behind bushes, barrels, and buildings whenever possible. He knew once he was inside no one could really bother him.

Alex purchased the least expensive breakfast on the menu and sat down in a corner of McDonald's to eat his breakfast and figure out his next move. He knew from past experience that the church was in the opposite direction of the Thompsons, with the old house being somewhere in the middle. He could make his way back to the church, hoping that Mrs. Thompson had not told the police about where he had stayed. His gut feeling was that she wouldn't have, but he didn't know if he dared to go there. Still, it was the safest place he had found in the time he had been roaming the city, and certainly better than returning again to the old house and taking a chance with the gang. Maybe he could just go check the church out from a distance and make sure the police weren't lurking nearby. He just didn't know if he should chance it.

After finishing off his breakfast, he decided he would clean up as best he could in the restroom and try to find a place nearby where he could hide if necessary. That way he would still be close enough to McDonald's if he needed to get inside. He would wait until it was closer to evening before heading toward the church. Surely the police would not be around at that time.

Alex used the restroom to clean up before he went outside and searched the area around the building. A short distance from the McDonald's there was a deserted school bus, sitting near a run-down garage. Glancing around quickly to make sure no one was in sight, Alex climbed into the bus to see if it would work as a place to stay until dark. Several of the seats toward the back of the bus had been ripped from the framework and the emergency exit door hung open, but if Alex pushed one of the cushions between two of the seats, he could sit or lie there virtually without being seen. Even if someone entered the bus, he would still have openings on both ends of the bus as escape routes if they spotted him. The area was only a couple of blocks or so from the McDonald's if he had to make a run for it. Alex quickly made the decision to stay and pushed the cushions into place, straining against the pain in his side where his ribs had not healed completely. By stacking two of them together, he made an area where he could actually curl up and sleep if he wanted to. Still, the thought of staying here after dark was not a pleasant one. He climbed up on the seat, used his backpack as a pillow, and lay there thinking about how close he had come to getting some help. He longed for the safety and warmth of the Thompsons but knew he could never go back. He had caused them enough trouble.

Before long the warmth of the bus combined with the meal and the short night's sleep had Alex dozing. He saw himself drifting on air out of the bus and into a house that was strange yet familiar at the same time. He saw the woman from his dreams laughing up at him for a moment, but then turning in terror as a man entered the room. He turned in that direction as well and the room went black. He blinked his eyes several time to bring the scene into focus and saw a gun lying on the floor. When he turned back to look at the woman, she was lying on the floor in a pool of blood. Alex floated there in helplessness, his tears falling down on her. Then the room went dark again and Alex was suddenly floating above the congregation at the church. The old priest was talking about Jesus dying on the cross for our sins. "Whose sins?" Alex wondered. Suddenly the priest seemed to be looking right and him and everyone else was looking up at him and pointing. Alex sat up with a start and felt the sweat beaded up on his forehead. He knew immediately that he had been dreaming again, but what did it all mean? Did he kill his own mother? Alex pulled his knees up to his chest and sobbed for all he was worth.

As night drew near, Alex made his way carefully to the outskirts of the church. He had purchased a sandwich and milk from McDonald's, which he clutched tightly in his hand, and hoped to find his way back to the relative safety of the bell tower. He saw no signs of police cars or anyone lingering near the entrance, so he decided to go for it. Without another moment of hesitation, fearing that he would lose his nerve at any second, he opened the door and quickly made his way to the back of the church. The church was unoccupied at this time of the day, and fairly dark except for the candles that always burned at the front near the altar. An aura of peace settled over Alex as he quietly made his way up the familiar staircases to the bell tower. He felt his way to the back of the room and opened the door of the storage area. Everything seemed to be in place, just as he had left it only the day before. Alex didn't bother to move anything this time. Leaving the door slightly ajar for air and light he sat on the edge of a cot and opened the bag. He devoured the sandwich. He drank the milk, stuffed the trash in the crumpled bag, and wadded it up like a ball. He climbed all the way onto the small cot and curled himself up as well, somewhat resembling the bag he had just dropped on the floor. He was back where he started weeks ago, with not much more than the clothes on his back.

Once again Alex drifted into an exhausted sleep. He found himself in a schoolroom setting, eagerly raising his hand to answer the question that the teacher had asked the class. Just as she was about to pick on Alex, the schoolroom door burst open and two police officers came in pointing fingers directly at him! Alex ran from the room, pushing past them and ended up in the room that he had stayed in at the Thompsons'. He was looking around the room in confusion when a lady tapped on the door and came in carrying a plate of cookies and a glass of milk. She sat them on the dresser and turned to Alex with outstretched arms. Without hesitating, Alex threw his arms around the woman, sobbing, "Mom!" Alex awoke with fresh tears on his face. He lay still for a moment, reliving the dream and what it meant. He knew for sure now that he was right. The lady he kept dreaming of was his mom. But if she was, then what about the dream he had on the bus? Had Alex really killed her? And what did he do now? Maybe he should have gone with the policemen. He closed his eyes tight and willed himself to go back to sleep. He wished for a brief moment, before real sleep claimed him, that this whole ordeal was just one long, ugly nightmare.

Daylight streamed into the room, and the warmth was at first comforting and then somewhat stifling. Alex lay on the cot wanting to stay there forever, but knowing that he would have to get up and go down to the restroom real soon. He uncurled his legs and sat up. He rubbed his side absently, where his ribs were still tender, wondering what was ahead of him today. He didn't really know which way to turn for sure. He knew that, eventually, at least Mrs. Thompson would check the church and find out that he was back here. He wished that she would walk in the door and tell him what to do. Before the thought even left his mind, he heard someone coming. Whoever it was walked slowly, making a slightly louder thump with one foot than the other. Alex held his breath wishing desperately for Mrs.

Thompson and knowing in his heart it wasn't her and he could be in for trouble. There was no escape, and not even enough time to hide. At this point he felt so depressed that he just didn't care.

The old pastor walked in the door and looked directly at Alex. Again Alex noticed the resemblance to the shadowy figure in the old house. He walked up to Alex and gently laid his hand on Alex's head. "Son," he said quietly, "please come with me."

Alex stood up without saying a word and followed the pastor. He had no fight left, nowhere to run, and no one who cared. The pastor led Alex down the stairs, up the aisle, past the altar, and into a small office. Noticing a restroom sign just outside the door, Alex stammered, "S-Sir, could I use the bathroom first?"

He motioned Alex to go ahead. As Alex left, he stood in the doorway wondering if he had made a mistake in letting him go, but within a few moments he heard Alex washing up and relaxed. When Alex came back into the office, the old priest motioned him to a chair and sat down facing him. First, he took both of Alex's hands and said, "Are you all right, son?"

Alex nodded.

"Look at me, son."

Alex lifted his chin and for the first time looked directly at the pastor. "I'm s-sorry," he told the priest, "I had nowhere else to go."

The pastor held up his hand to stop Alex from saying anything further. "Son, I know all about you. I've been praying for you for weeks, watching out for you when I could. When you left the bell tower, I was worried, so I have been watching for you. I saw you and Mrs. Thompson leaving here a couple of days ago, so I thought you must be staying with them. Then their son David came by yesterday to see me and explained some of what happened with the police and all and that you were on the run again. We all hoped you would come back here so we could help you. Yes, I know them," he said at Alex's look of surprise. "David and his wife Heather actually attend here. The last month or so Heather has gotten so big with child that she can't sit that long, but this is their church, son. I know that the Thompsons have been caring for you, and they told me about the trouble with the gang and your escape. When you overheard them arguing with the police and ran away, Mrs. Thompson was sure that eventually you would come back here. However, she did not tell the police. She simply asked me to watch for you and contact her if you returned."

Alex nodded, miserable.

"They are on the way here to pick you up, son, and"—at Alex's startled yet somewhat relieved expression—"I believe that they have some good news for you. I will let them tell you themselves," he finished as Mr. and Mrs. Thompson rushed in the door.

Several hours away, in Grand Rapids, Michigan, a woman sat quietly on the edge of her son's bed, holding a framed picture that showed the two of them laughing at the camera with their faces painted like silly clowns. *Oh, Matthew*, she thought sadly, *where are you*? Tears trailed slowly down her cheeks and fell silently on the picture. She recalled the previous Halloween when she and Matt had been so excited with fall and getting ready for the church party. They had baked cookies to take and Matt was so happy! He was such a bright, intelligent little boy. She reached over to place the photo back on the dresser and winced at the pain in her shoulder. She adjusted her arm in the sling to rest more comfortably and wished for the thousandth time that she had never met Alex Johnson. How had she ever gotten mixed up with the likes of that man and, even worse, not realized just how devious he and his friends really were? He had fooled her with his act of concern for her and Matt, and she had ignored the signs along the way telling her it was too good to be true. Still, how could he have gone along with anyone hurting a little boy? Did he know that one of the men had a gun and planned to kill her? They must have taken Matt so he couldn't identify them. Did they still have him? Was he safe? If only she had not passed out and hit her head when she had fallen, she would have been there to save Matt. She knew that the man with the gun had hit Matt on the back of the head when he ran to help her. Dejectedly she bowed her head and the tears fell softly on the carpet. “Dear God, she prayed, please keep Matt safe until I can find him. Please bring him home to me. Please God, please.”

20

GOOD NEWS!

Mrs. Thompson rushed in and snatched Alex out of the chair. "Oh, Alex," she said. "I have been so worried!" She threw her arms around Alex and hugged him so tight that he flinched in pain!

Mr. Thompson walked over and put an arm around the two of them. "You gave us quite a scare, Alex," he stated.

The old pastor stood up and headed to the door. "You all need time to talk," he stated quietly. "I will be right outside. You are safe here, so take as much time as you need."

The Thompsons looked at the old priest and smiled. Mr. Thompson walked over and extended his hand. "Thank you, John," he said with a smile. "Thank you!" He closed the door to the small office, pulled up another chair, and said, "Sit down, both of you." Alex looked from one to the other with anxiety but could not get one word out of his mouth. Mr. Thompson pulled a wrinkled newspaper clipping out of his pocket and spread it out on the desk in front of them. "Alex," he started, "I have been doing some research since the day you washed all of the windows in my store. I started with Chicago and the outlaying cities here in Illinois, and finally made it to the closest cities in Michigan. Once I got there, I hit pay dirt."

"I d-don't understand, sir," Alex stammered.

"Tell him what you mean!" Mrs. Thompson exclaimed.

"Hold on there, Tilly," Mr. Thompson replied, "just give me a minute, here. Alex," he went on, "let me explain myself. I was searching through newspapers online, through local libraries, looking for anything that would have involved a missing boy. Then the police came by the other night, and I started looking even harder! I knew you could not have always been around this area or I would have noticed you before. You were so out of place here it was obvious that there was more to your story." At this point Mr. Thompson smiled at Alex and patted his head before he prepared to continue.

Mrs. Thompson couldn't stand it another moment. She turned to Alex and took both his hands in her own and said without further ado, "Alex, we think we found your mom!"

Alex jumped to his feet and looked from Mrs. Thompson to Mr. Thompson. "W-where, is she?" he stammered. "Is she alive?"

"What do you mean, son," Mr. Thompson replied, "of course she's alive. She's been looking for you for weeks, ever since she got out of the hospital." Mrs. Thompson gave Mr. Thompson a warning look, but Mr. Thompson pointed to the newspaper clipping once again. "Look, son, look at what it says."

Alex finally took a good look at the newspaper clipping. Staring out of the page was the woman that Alex had seen over and over in his dreams, the one that he had felt must be his mother. As he looked at the picture, tears began to slide down his cheeks. He read the caption: "Mother shot, searches for eleven-year-old son." Alex blinked rapidly, but he couldn't clear the tears away fast enough to read the article. Mrs. Thompson picked up the paper and began to read. "The young woman in Grand Rapids, Michigan, who was shot in her home almost two months ago, continues searching for her son who was abducted during the altercation. Young Matthew Zachary Alan was with his mother at the time of shooting. Three men broke into the home, took money and valuables, and attempted to get the keys to the woman's car. When the woman resisted, she was shot and hit her head as she fell to the floor, rendering herself unconscious. When she came to, she crawled to the phone and dialed 911, before she again lost consciousness. The police arrived and were able to get her to the hospital where she remained for almost a month, with a gunshot wound to the shoulder and a concussion. Her son has been missing since that night. Now that she has been released from the hospital, she has been instrumental in a state-wide search for her son. Matthew is four foot six, and has sandy-brown hair and hazel eyes. He was last seen in an old denim shirt and jeans and sneakers. If you have any information on this case, please call the silent observer at 616-777-4357." Below the picture of his mom was a picture of him that looked like a school picture.

Mrs. Thompson dropped the clipping and put her arms around the now-sobbing boy. "I'm M-Matt," she heard him mumble, and tears slid down her cheeks as well. "My name is M-Matt."

Mr. Thompson once again placed his arms around both of them. Once Matt had recovered from the initial shock, he reached down and picked up the paper. "Shall we call your mom, son?" he asked Matt.

Gabrielle Alan stood in her kitchen trying to find the energy to open the fridge and force herself to prepare something to eat. She had no appetite at all but knew that she had to eat in order to keep up her strength and help in the search for Matt. She pulled out butter and cheese for a grilled cheese sandwich just as her cell phone rang. Setting the food on the counter, she answered her phone as God answered her prayers.

"Mrs. Alan?" a pleasant voice questioned.

"Yes," she replied cautiously, "can I help you?"

Mr. Thompson handed the phone to Matt. "M-mom," Matt said hesitantly.

Gabrielle almost dropped the phone. "Matt," she started to sob, "is that you, honey?"

"Yes, M-mom, it's me, please don't cry!"

Gabrielle pulled on every ounce of strength she had and answered more calmly, "Oh, Matt! Are you okay?"

"Yes, yes I am," Matt replied. "Where are you? When can I see you? Are you really okay? I thought I killed you!" Suddenly Matt's stuttering was gone, replaced by feverish excitement.

"I'm home, honey. Where are you? I'll come and get you right now. Who are you with?" Matt was starting to cry again. After all the weeks of being tough and taking care of himself, suddenly he was acting like a little boy again. Mr. Thompson took the phone from him, as he collapsed in Mrs. Thompson's arms.

21

HOME AT LAST!

Matt could hear Mr. Thompson's voice in the background as he stood crying against Mrs. Thompson. She patted his back and tried to console him, but everything was zooming into his brain like a race car. His mother's voice had brought it all rushing back. Matt was remembering all sorts of things… dancing around wearing the old clothes that his mom was boxing up for Good Will, while he grabbed them and put them on, insisting they still fit him. One minute they had been laughing at how much he was growing and the next they were startled by someone banging on the door. Matt remembered his mom checking the locked door and then running for him as the men came crashing into the house. He saw her new boyfriend Alex and his friends and watched them stomping around grabbing their things and shoving his mother out of the way. He saw her clutching her purse until one of the men snatched it away from her. Then he heard the loud bang and saw her lying on the floor as he had in his dream with her blood pooling around her. He saw Alex over his shoulder as he ran for her and heard her scream, "Alex, no!" Then he felt a crushing blow on the back of his head, the stifling feeling as something was thrown over his head and then nothing. Alex blinked the memories away as Mrs. Thompson tried to comfort him, but the tears would not stop. Looking up at her, he noticed that Mrs. Thompson was crying too.

As Mr. Thompson hung up the phone, Alex finally stood back from Mrs. Thompson. As if in a trance, he reached up and began rubbing the back of his head where the wound could still be felt today. It was all *almost* too much for him. Mr. Thompson had given his mother directions, and as he turned toward him, Matt reached out a hand to him. Anxiously he asked, "Is she coming?"

"Of course she is, son," Mr. Thompson replied. He took Matt's hand in both of his. "Let's get out of here and go home and wait for her."

As the three of them came out of the door, the old pastor stood up from where he had been kneeling at the altar. The Thompsons led Matt over to where he stood. He looked at Matt standing there and softly placed a hand on his shoulder. "The Lord has been with you, son," he said quietly. "Let's pray, shall we?" Matt was too excited to hear much of the prayer, but the Thompsons clutched hands and listened to every word. "Lord, thank you for the gift of your son and the many blessings you provide daily. Thank you for the Thompsons and for young Matthew. Thank you for his mother's love and the faith that kept her ever on the path that led us to finding her. Keep her safe as she travels to reconnect with her son at last. Be with them all, Lord, as they begin a new chapter in their lives. Thank you for knowing each of us by name, and for giving us all the miracle of hope. Amen."

"Home," Matt thought, "I'm really going home!"

> Yes, he didn't look like much in his dirty, tattered clothes
> His fingernails were filthy and he had a runny nose…
> … And who would ever even try to reach this child, and find a clue
> Responding to his soundless cry and sticking by to see him through
> Would you?

I hope you would! Thank you, Thompsons! The Lord be with you all!

EPILOGUE

The young priest looked out at the congregation with a feeling of awe. Almost twenty years ago, this church had been his safe haven. Now it was his home, family, and responsibility. A sense of belonging came over him, and he realized how much it all meant to him. This church had once given him the hope and safety he needed at a desperate point in his life, and he was determined to give it back, to give that sense of hope and safety to others. A bit of sadness crept in as he remembered the recent death of Pastor John, but he knew the old priest would appreciate that Matt had come back to the church that had protected him. He had watched over Matt and now Matt would watch over his congregation and pay it forward. He noticed Dr. David and his wife Heather, along with their three growing children. Mr. and Mrs. Thompson were there as well, a bit frailer now but so proud to be part of "his" congregation. He smiled, remembering their care and kindness. Mr. Thompson had insisted on giving him the money he got from the old coins he discovered in the first mountain of "stuff" he had moved for him, to use for his education. Matt would never forget it. He would never forget *him*. He saw his mother near the front, the lady of his dreams. Those dreams had also given him comfort and hope. His mom had moved to Chicago recently to be near him. She too was grateful for this church and all it had meant to her son and to helping her find him. The past was finally behind them, and justice had been served to Alex and his friends long ago. She and Matthew had grown closer to God and to each other over the past years, and the number of people they had touched as a result was significant. They understood the depth of despair in being deceived and lost. And they understood the utter joy of being found. They believed it was all connected to faith in God. So they encouraged others, now, to believe. To know that no matter what God is always there for you. Every person matters in this life, and everyone deserves a chance. A chance to be who God created them to be.

❧

Please reach out when you see someone in need. Don't be afraid to help, because "…what seemed hopeless at a glance, was a very special child indeed, and given just a single chance, one other who would see his need the "real him" might be born…"

Because God was ever present, because the Thompsons cared, because his mother never stopped praying, the "real"

Matthew was discovered, and he became a beacon of light to others. You see, you never know how many lives you may impact with one simple act of kindness. God Bless you.

CPSIA information can be obtained
at www.ICGtesting.com
Printed in the USA
BVOW11s0559260816
460229BV00002B/4/P